THE DEATHBRINGER

Manfred von Conta's first novel is not only a study in depth of
the psychotic make-up of a killer but also a devastating condemnation of a society that is able to shrug off the smoke signals
for help from the mentally sick—the would-be murderers. Xaver
Ykdrasil Zangl, owner of a lending library in Vienna, lives a
lonely, secluded life among his books, avoiding human contact
and improving his mind. A stomach upset causes him to visit a
local doctor whose medicaments prove ineffective. Dr. Kralicek,
aware of the psychologically disturbed condition of the patient,
decides to apply some psycho-analysis himself.

This course of psycho-therapy brings out the latent pathological
symptoms in Zangl. Anxious to create some order in the chaos
of his drives, wishes, lusts he starts to keep a diary. Early loss
of the father figure leads to his identification with Dr. Kralicek,
to the fixation on the doctor in his role as magician, and almost
to the doctor's murder. A desperate bid for a trace of reality to
penetrate his consciousness drives Zangl to kill first a prostitute
who was unwilling to conform with his distorted picture of her
and later, one of his clients, a homosexual lawyer who buys up
his stock of pornography. In both cases Zangl is convinced of
having destroyed evil. Eventually he suspects the doctor of plot-
ting against him and with that his mental death sets in. He locks
himself in his room and his insane cries and hammerings are
shamefacedly ignored by the neighbours. At last it is the land-
lord, eager for his rent, who takes action : Zangl is tried and put
away in a state asylum.

THE DEATHBRINGER

a novel by
MANFRED VON CONTA

translated from the German by
EVA FIGES

CALDER & BOYARS · LONDON

First published in Great Britain 1971
by Calder and Boyars Ltd
18 Brewer Street London W1R 4AS

Originally published 1969 as Der Totmacher
by Diogenes Verlag AG Zurich

ISBN 0 7145 0807 1 cloth edition

ISBN 0 7145 0876 4 paper edition

Printed in Great Britain by
Clarke, Doble & Brendon Ltd, Plymouth

1

THE FIRST time Xaver Ykdrasil Zangl consulted Doctor Kralicek, he was totally unaware of the magic power which (according to Zangl) he exerted over him later. It was, as I was able to discover in my capacity as reporter on the case, a morning in May, the sky was blue, when the thirty-three-year-old Zangl locked up his lending library in order to go and see the doctor. He had been having digestive trouble for some time, and in fact there appeared to be no ascertainable reason why he should have gone to see a doctor on that particular day. He was not getting real pains, just a constant, dull feeling in his stomach that made him tired and listless and stopped him thinking clearly. He told the doctor that he felt as though he were living "under a cloud".

Dr. Kralicek's surgery was only five minutes' walk from the lending library, and Zangl had noticed it because every morning on his way to work he passed the enamel plate which had been fixed high up by the entrance to one of the gaunt grey tenement houses. It is only tourists who think Vienna "beautiful". Large areas of the city consist of old tenement houses built close together during the last century. Fat children with pale faces play in the dark courtyards, insofar as there are any children at all. The majority of the population in the twisted streets of these large areas of the city between the Ringstrasse and the outskirts are old people, especially old women who have to make do on a meagre pension. They walk along the alleyways leading overfed old dogs who look as mangy as their owners, alleyways devoid

of a single tree or blade of grass, without a trace of green
vegetation. Just asphalt, paving stones, tramlines and dark
courtyards where dustbins stand.

After leaving the street Zangl had to cross three such
courtyards to get to the doctor's surgery. As we know from
his diary, in the last courtyard the air rang with the forceful
voice of a woman calling out numbers loudly and slowly,
with the steadiness of a dripping tap. She remained invisible,
but must have been sitting somewhere up there behind an
open window. The numbers that accompanied Zangl on his
way were high ones.

But after crossing the third courtyard he reached a garden.
The high fire-proof walls made of red bricks, which enclosed
the garden, were covered with ivy right up to the eaves, so
that Dr. Kralicek's little house seemed to be resting in a box
of green satin. Neatly trimmed rosebushes grew round the
house and ramblers climbed up a trellis against the friendly
walls, which were painted a pale ochre. In the garden the
woman's voice could no longer be heard counting, but
sparrows twittered, and a thin straight column of white
smoke rose out of the chimney, between the ivy-clad walls,
and up to the blue sky.

Xaver Zangl was very pleased that he had overcome his
shyness and had come to see the doctor. Normally he avoided
contact with other people. In the shop it was another
matter. He did not regard customers as human beings, but
simply as customers, and he only spoke briefly to them. The
customers he liked best were those that already knew the
title of the book they wanted to borrow. They named the
title and he went to fetch the book from the shelves whilst
they silently filled in the index card he had pushed towards
them. He knew that many customers, who would have liked
a chat about books or neighbours with him, were put off by
his taciturn manner and did not come back. But this did not
bother him. Thanks to his legacy he was not dependent on

the income from his library and had, in fact, only taken it over two years earlier in order to have some peace and quiet for his hobbies.

When he saw the garden and the little yellow house set amidst the rosebushes he suddenly felt light-hearted and gay, and he looked forward to being able to talk to the doctor about himself—Xaver Ykdrasil Zangl—a clearly defined person, whose life showed clear contours and a firm structure dictated by time, profession and government concessions. For, since he had owned the library, he had allowed all his old acquaintanceships to fall by the wayside, he forgot these people as though they had never existed. He had become solitary. He wanted loneliness, because this alone left his mind free to roam in a way which he had so often longed for during the years he had spent as book-keeper in a small workshop producing plastic goods. Even now he called this workshop, in which eight workers pressed out buckets, tubs, beakers and such-like from plastic powder delivered by the sack, "the factory", and he still loathed the memory of it, so that he avoided thinking about it as far as possible. To him it seemed a heavy burden which had dragged him down to the banality of an insubstantial reality for many precious years of his life. But now that he was free it sometimes seemed to him as though there was no reality at all, not even the higher one he used to long for so much. Then he was suffused by a sense of profound emptiness, and sat between his bookshelves with a glassy stare and sluggish pulse, whilst his imagination constructed all kinds of obscene images. Greedily he devoured large mouthfuls of bread and black pudding, until he began to feel sick.

He mentioned this diet to Dr. Kralicek as the probable cause of his complaint. He chatted gaily on, as though he did not take himself and his illness very seriously. And yet he got a feeling of well-being from the concern he detected in Dr. Kralicek, as the latter thoughtfully ran his cool fingers over the abdomen of his patient, who lay stretched out on a couch. This solemnity made him feel that he was in good, considerate hands, that he did not have to worry any more, on the contrary, he could be as happy as a lark. Because if he did not worry, simply asked cynically: "Something wrong with my intestines?" this higher authority remained to shield him from harm. It now advised him to eat regularly, cooked meals only.

Unfortunately this was not possible, Xaver Zangl explained, and with a little laugh he added, that he was, so to speak, a victim of his profession, since he could not warm up a meal whilst the library was open. He was much more likely to snatch a bite whilst nobody happened to be there, and even when he was eating he had to be prepared for a customer to demand his attention. According to Dr. Kralicek's report he twice mentioned the "traffic" at the lending library, and once he described it as "hectic"—no doubt in order to evoke sympathy in the listener, and heighten his concern with this touch of human sympathy. But Dr. Kralicek only answered, it couldn't be that hectic at lunchtime in the lending library, in any case Zangl should certainly make sure he had something hot, with a low fat content, in the evening. Was he married?

Zangl hesitated for a moment before he answered, because the question caught him unprepared. He had not thought about his marriage, which had ended in divorce two years before, for a long time. Now he just said: "Was. No, I cook for myself in the evening."

The doctor thought this did not matter, Zangl could perfectly well cook himself some lean meat, a few vegetables, or any easily digestible sweet like rice pudding or semolina.

While the doctor sat at his desk, making out a prescription for pills he was to take three times a day, Zangl thought about his visit to the doctor, the course it had taken. He was satisfied.

Immediately on his arrival Zangl, who had a clear recollection of the words "All insurance patients" added to the enamel plate, had stressed that he was coming as a private patient. He did not want to be a mere receipt, a faceless number. The doctor had laughed and said that all people were alike as far as he was concerned, private or insurance, the only difference was in the book-keeping. For a moment Xaver Zangl tensed inwardly in protest at the idea of being put on the same level as other anonymous people, but the idea that the doctor was obviously not thinking selfishly about how much money he could make out of him, that he was prepared to accept each patient as an individual, and the experience of his careful examination methods satisfied Xaver Zangl, particularly as Doctor Kralicek asked him to drop in again in a week's time. He warned Zangl to follow his advice scrupulously, and added that although there was nothing to worry about at the moment, such intestinal trouble could easily lead to an ulcer, perhaps even cancer. Zangl left in high spirits: here was someone who thought about him, who would not immediately forget him, who wanted to see him again in a week's time. The world had, if I may be allowed to try and summarise Xaver Zangl's lengthy description in his diary of his feelings as he crossed the three courtyards, lost something of its threatening strangeness, it had acquired shape, had become tangible and comprehensible. During the next few days Zangl read with great interest, in the quiet hours spent between his bookshelves, a hefty history of the Jewish people, made notes, and relished the steady way he turned over the pages. He did not waste any time thinking about the third bookcase, which was hidden behind a curtain in the corner, because he did not need to.

The third bookcase contained pornographic books and was

one of the reasons why Zangl had taken over the library when he unexpectedly found himself with enough money to be able to give up the restricting business of earning his daily bread.

For he felt curiously cramped by having to work to the routine of office hours: on the one hand the daily confrontation with other people forced him to adapt to their world, to more or less conform in the way he thought, spoke and felt. Each of them had a place in their respective families, they all regarded certain moral laws as unquestionably right, even when they broke them on occasion, and they behaved like all their neighbours. But in Xaver Zangl there was something that wanted to grow and proliferate beyond all bounds, something that he could not give a name to, but which he sometimes described as "black" or "sinister" when he felt it dully within himself. It was something very strong, demanding, which sometimes took his breath away and made him hate the world about him, since it stopped him from allowing it to grow and develop freely. But this dark thing encroached on the edge of his consciousness in many different ways. At first he was made aware of it by the fact that he found the jokes and diversions of his workmates stupid, empty, banal, meaningless and silly. Over and over again he noticed contradictions in their thought processes, and he despised them because they made life so comfortable for themselves with these inanities. But at the same time he was also dissatisfied with himself, because he realised that his own intellect was inadequately trained and that he lacked the rich vocabulary necessary to give expression to the truths (or what he regarded as the truths) which he would have liked to hurl at his fellow human beings. Sometimes he felt that, the way he appeared in his surroundings, he was in fact only a part of a much bigger, more significant personality, and he longed for union with this other person, without really knowing how he could get closer to him. The library

—so he thought—would give him an opportunity to attain, through industrious and attentive reading, what he called "higher insight", or simply a state of "loftiness", without his being able to think of a better name for this either.

But the dark thing had another side to it, a side which pulled Zangl away from his high ideals, dragged him down into the abyss. It expressed itself in bold erotic fantasies, the realisation of which he regarded as shameful, to be severely condemned. Compared to the pleasure which these illusory images seemed to promise him, being with his wife was an insipid, boring, ultimately repulsive occupation, and merely to think about it made him bad-tempered and morose. He also believed that his wife only had intercourse with him out of cold calculation, in order to gain possession of him, just like the members of the narrow-minded fraternity who forced him to do his duty.

He left his wife, hoping that he would be able to enjoy a rich and colourful love life, of which she alone, through her existence, had so far deprived him, but during the year that followed their separation he had not succeeded in finding suitable partners. His own shyness, a timidity which he himself thought petty, hindered him, more than awareness of his unhealthily bloated appearance, from bringing about even the most fleeting sexual contact, even when he had, blushing and stammering, persuaded some woman or other to spend an evening with him at the cinema or in a restaurant. He was extremely annoyed with himself about this obstructive feeling of guilt, but ultimately he blamed his environment for the state of discontent in which he was forced to live. Was it not this environment, full of such despicable oafs, which had burdened him with these tormenting fetters of a narrow morality, since it forced him to conform in order to earn his daily bread?

When, after the death of his aunt, Xaver Zangl could enjoy his inheritance, he escaped from this environment with a great sense of relief, for two reasons: on the one hand he was now free, his mind, unhampered by everyday banality, could turn to "loftiness", on the other hand he could turn his attention to "low things", namely the pleasure of pornographic pictures, without being constantly reminded by his surroundings that what he was doing was "low".

During the first few months of his new existence as the owner of a lending library "loftiness" still ruled the day; he devoured all sorts of philosophical literature, without always having an exact understanding of what he had read, but at least he had the intoxicating feeling of coming into contact with knowledge for the first time since he had prematurely broken off his high school studies out of laziness and a fear of life. Human beings, while he was so engaged, vanished from his recollection as fast as the landscape shrinks beneath the eyes of a bird of prey. But imperceptibly the balance of his thoughts shifted from the fifth bookcase, in which the philosophers stood, to the third, which he had taken over from his predecessor with a beating heart, but without looking at it.

When Xaver Zangl sought out Dr. Kralicek on account of a gastric disorder, his thoughts had not been turned to "loftiness" for a long time; he had fallen victim to the third bookcase, which did not activate his bad conscience to any great extent, since he had left behind and almost forgotten the standards of behaviour in the world of regular work.

Now, since we know what happened to Zangl in the end, a review of the last months compels one to think that, driven by a powerful force beyond his control, he cut himself off from his environment, in that he first abandoned his wife, then his job, buried himself in the library and there chased away his customers—his last contact with the outside world —by his unsocial behaviour. No longer forced to adapt himself socially to his place of work, Zangl seems to have lost the restraining influence that saved him, which had up to that time made it possible for him to keep the dark side in check. When he came to Dr. Kralicek's surgery the dark side had already gained the upper hand, the dissolution of his personality structure was in full spate, and it seems to me that the dull pains which Zangl complained about were nothing other than a cry for help, which the "normal" person in Zangl, already completely vanquished by the "darkness", tried to get past the warder and smuggle to the surface. It must be left to the judgement of the commission whether Zangl was asking too much of Kralicek, since the doctor did not recognise these appeals for help as such in the first instance. In addition, only the commission can judge whether he was acting negligently in not considering the patient as a possible danger to the general public, when he did begin to suspect the causes of Zangl's harmless physical ailment.

I shall endeavour to make my report as conscientious as possible, relying in the first instance on Kralicek's memory, but later also on the detailed entries which Zangl himself made in his diary. I must point out to the commission right at the start that in spite of all my attempts at the utmost objectivity, very many connections must be a matter of conjecture on my part, and it is only possible to speculate on how these should be interpreted. For example, the assumption that Zangl's visit to Dr. Kralicek was a kind of appeal for help on the part of Zangl's personality, subjugated by destructive drives, is decisive for the assessment of the responsibility with which Dr. Kralicek unexpectedly found himself confronted, but it is difficult to prove. However, this assumption is supported by Zangl's extraordinary behaviour after the two murders, which also leads one to suspect that, with the desperation of a drowning man, he only killed in order to raise the alarm and bring about his own rescue by the outside world. Why otherwise did he behave in a manner which would inevitably put the police on his tracks?

Well, I do not wish to anticipate your own conclusions, and in the following pages I will report dispassionately and, as far as is possible without loss of comprehension, allow Zangl to speak for himself through his diary.

2

To begin with there was a temporary improvement in Zangl's condition in the week following his first visit to the doctor, but as the days passed Zangl slid back into his old ways, his lively interest in the history of the Jewish people subsided, the third case occupied the forefront of his consciousness as it had before, his indigestion returned, and he was once more subject to the old, dull restlessness which made him go out in the evening, on the pretext of a little walk, leave his flat and direct his steps, as though under a magic spell, towards the part of town where prostitutes walk the streets.

Finally he welcomed the prospect of another visit to the doctor, which he thought would do him good. On the subject of this second visit he later noted in his diary:

"The same enchantment as on the first occasion, when I walked through the courtyards and stepped into the rose garden: another world. My heart thudded as though I had come very close to a secret. He is very calm. Hardly moves when he talks. His white coat, the steady gleam of his spectacles, his round head, almost bald. He sits in front of the window, so that it is difficult to make out his face. But I could see the lines: leftover traces of spiritual adventures. His surgery is dominated by sober white, nickel-plated metal, washable synthetics. A cold world. But only on the surface. Through the crack of a half-open door, I noticed the dark spines of a mass of books. I took to him at once because he is a reader. Because I read a lot too."

So even during that second visit Zangl felt that there was a secret bond between him and Dr. Kralicek. At first it was only a feeling that they had interests in common, but later on it grew, as we know, to this fantastic mania, which might have cost the doctor his life too. For the time being, of course, in spite of his growing awareness of a mysterious union, he was still coldly distant, and did not hesitate to present his health card, in spite of the fact that he had registered as a private patient, after he realised that in this practice no distinction was made between private and panel patients, so that he could expect the doctor's unstinting sympathy without any financial sacrifice.

He was not disappointed. The doctor showed his continuing interest by asking him what the Christian name "Ykdrasil" meant, and his interest in him increased when he found that he was unable to answer promptly and clearly; on the contrary, he became embarrassed, and no doubt it was at this stage that the doctor began to suspect some mental disturbance, because the sick man appeared to have forgotten everything relating to his family, his origins, his profession and early life, and could only produce fragmentary information after intense concentration. From Zangl's stuttered words Dr. Kralicek did, however, manage to make out that his father appeared to have been a member of a union devoted to the cultivation of Teutonic usage and that the name Ykdrasil had something to do with Nordic mythology. Shortly after Zangl's birth his father had left wife and child to devote himself entirely to one of those militant political movements active at that time. No more was heard of him. Zangl reported this fact as though it was some piece of fabled lore from another planet which had absolutely nothing to do with his own person.

Contrary to the statement he made later, Dr. Kralicek does seem to have decided to treat his patient's complaint as psychosomatic in origin. But he did nothing about it until

Xaver Zangl called to see him a third time, because he decided to go on treating him with medicine for the time being, and hope for a possible improvement. But when, after a lapse of another week, Xaver Zangl went on complaining about cramps, indigestion and yellowish stools, the doctor must have started considering a psychoanalytic approach. The enthusiasm with which Zangl greeted this proposal, the professional curiosity of the practitioner, who was eager to gain first-hand experience of symptoms only familiar to him from textbooks, the fact that the patient seemed sensible and the apparently superficial nature of his disturbance, from which an unpractised eye could not have deduced the seriousness of his case—probably all these factors combined to make Dr. Kralicek take the fateful decision to try his hand, just this once, at an area of therapy usually reserved for his psychiatric colleagues.

Immediately after this first analytic session Xaver Zangl began to keep a diary. Dr. Kralicek, I would like to remind you, did not know anything about this manuscript, as, indeed, much else that we know—since we are in possession of Zangl's notes—remained unknown to him, so that it is easier for us to judge what was going on in Zangl's mind. But we can also see from this manuscript with what refinement the sick man veiled his true self from the doctor's eyes, without totally concealing it. I repeat what I said earlier: the suppressed "normal person" in Zangl tried, over and over again, throughout the period of his contact with the doctor, to smuggle messages out of his dungeon in order to effect a rescue from his prison. At the same time, however, the power that controlled Zangl's conscious mind tried to suppress these messages.

In his diary Zangl wrote:

"Keeping a diary is a strange thing. You chase after events with your tongue hanging out and never catch up with them. I feel as though I could roll out an enormous quantity of material, as though I could go on writing for hours and hours—and suddenly the wind goes out of my sails. I sit at the table, the lamp burning above me, and my thoughts have vanished. Have slipped away like runaway horses. I must tell Dr. K. about these phenomena at all costs.

Yesterday he asked whether I had a full life. Thought about it, though K. and I have already discussed it. I saw myself in countless situations, sitting here at the table—and couldn't catch up with my writing. Then I drew until the evening. I'm an inventor *manqué*: yesterday it was a circuit diagram for remote control switch gear. The problem was, on the one hand to achieve a noiseless reaction, so that the people being spied on would not notice anything, on the other hand to operate two switches simultaneously with one signal. Namely divising a simple circuit for microphone and amplifier and also for the emission of regular impulses for the camera. A precondition for this arrangement is being able to obtain a camera which winds on automatically. It must also work without making a noise.

What would the materials for apparatus of that sort cost? The transmitter can be as large as you like, but the receiver? I suppose miniature receivers are very expensive. And what would I answer, if the dealer asked me what I wanted it for?

But the notes on K. are more important. I'm always in danger of losing myself. That's the consequence of having so many sides to one!

Of course I have a full life. I'm never bored. That's because of my nature. I have too many interests. For instance, I'm an amateur radio enthusiast.

'Radio—really?' asked K.

He knows me.

I'm not really a radio enthusiast, only on paper. Just in the mind. Fiddling about with real equipment—whatever it's called—I don't go in for that. I don't have enough time. And being occupied with real things diverts too much attention from the consideration of abstract principles. Which is why I don't sit at the window, where things going on in the street would distract me, but behind the bookshelves.

'You want to dream—not live.'

This sentence struck me like the blow of a hammer. He revealed just what an exceptional person he is. How we resemble each other. His gaze penetrates the surface of things. I was silent for a while. This is what is so exceptional about K., that he has a magic gift for expressing things that have not been put into words before. He makes things take shape for me, until just the right expression wells up inside me. He gives me clarity of vision. This is what I felt quite distinctly at that moment. He is a magician. I shall call him Laurin. K. lives in a rose garden too. Yes, it really makes me happy, being able to call him Laurin. As Laurin he belongs only to me.

Until this moment I had never become conscious of the contrast between dreams and life. Even now I had doubts.

'I try to live dreams,' I corrected Laurin. He gave a warm laugh. Nothing seems to upset him.

'We'll talk about that tomorrow,' he said. 'My patients are waiting.' I left him feeling happy and elated. He wants to see me again tomorrow, I thought to myself. And: he doesn't regard me as a patient, not if he sends me away with the remark: 'My patients are waiting.' Or he would have said: 'The other patients are waiting.' I'm someone special to him. So our relationship is on a higher level than that of other people. A secret bond binds us together!

After that I shut up shop, so that I could make my entries undisturbed. Before I broke off to go for my walk, the local magistrate arrived. He knocked and shook the door, would not go away. I watched him through the bookshelves. A loathsome individual. He's only interested in the third bookcase. Filthy mind. I didn't let him in. That afternoon I was not in the mood for the third case. In fact I was furious with him for reminding me that I had a third bookcase. I found it an embarrassment. What would Laurin say, if he knew about it! And I only went out for walks to test myself. I took the same route as always, but I didn't so much as look. I didn't mind looking the other way. When I got home I even wished I had gone another way. Yesterday evening was the fifteenth day of my acquaintance with Laurin. But when the magistrate disturbed me I had only got as far as writing about my third visit to him. I must write much faster! When I got to Laurin the next day, he had a shocking revelation for me. He wants money from me!

He immediately hastened to explain to me the nature of my *illness*. My difficulties stem from unresolved tensions, which cannot be relieved with pills or powders. 'We could go on trying for months,' he said genially, 'but it wouldn't help. We could take your appendix out, and you'd feel better, because any opening of the abdomen makes the patient feel better. But it would soon come back. Let's get to the root of the matter.'

I agreed. The session costs a hundred schillings. And I pay him willingly. He has stirred such a wealth of ideas in me. I have an inkling of the deep insight to which he will lead me. As the days pass I regret the money less and less. It really pays.

People turn up their noses at neurotics and have no idea what a neurosis is. It just means that I haven't adapted. I've always said that there were many sides to me. Well, Laurin is saying the same thing in different words. He is offering me untold riches, kind as he is. Nobody has dreams like me. Any film is a load of rubbish in comparison. They are so significant! If I could find time to write them down, I'd be famous overnight!

But first of all I must take a provisional hold of this wealth.

I note down my dreams in a special exercise book for the purpose, using key words only. Later, when I have time, I shall have to transfer them, writing them out in full.

Because Laurin said, on my fourth visit, after we had sorted out the financial side—this distasteful talk about sordid money—that we should start with the outer circumstances of my personal life. Afterwards we could see how we got on from there. And I was to watch my dreams!

He is a magician. I never used to dream before. But now, the very first night, such an intoxicating dream: it's in the exercise book as number one. The story of how I search for my son all over the world—it gave me such a shock to realise that I had forgotten my son, that I woke up with a start and only dreamt the sequel when I went back to sleep—and finally found a photograph of him. A dock worker in Yokohama is holding it in his hand like a playing card. And it shows *me*! I was so excited that I wanted to rush over and see Laurin first thing in the morning, to tell him about it. But I restrained myself. I waited for the appointed time. Laurin just smiled when I told him about it.

'We'll talk about your dreams later.' That smile, how calm he is! His calmness makes me see myself objectively, step out of my own skin and look at myself, calms me down. I see more clearly. I am so grateful! Instead of discussing the dream, we talked about my mother: a hard-working, honest individual. She kept us both by working as a housekeeper in a hotel. She's dead now. Poor mummy! She was so energetic, so strong! Laurin is understanding. He nods at everything I say, as though he had known about it all along. He only interrupts with some simple question when I'm in danger of getting lost. He doesn't even take notes! I'd like to tell him everything. Absolutely *everything*!

Once he answered a remark of mine with a smile: 'I don't either.' This glimpse of a small part of his existence makes me really happy. It is difficult for me to remain matter-of-fact. I am always cool and matter-of-fact with Laurin. I keep the distance prescribed by him. I am worthy of him!

This is the extraordinary thing about my relationship with Laurin, that he understands everything right away, almost as though he had known it all along. I only have to give him key words, and he says 'I see'. Which is why we never waste time on boring details. We skip through the essentials at top speed. If only this journey could last for ever!

Only the essentials on the subject of my broken marriage, too. I'm not one of those divorced men who blame their wives for everything. On the contrary: it was all my fault. Because *she* was not out of the ordinary, I was!

If I had been as mediocre as her the marriage might have been very happy. But as it was, I demanded too much. I am very unusual in other ways too. Laurin understands. I don't have to explain anything to him. To put it in a nutshell, I was more or less dead. My sated, contented wife smothered me with her animal womb. Yes, like an animal. Even the way she licked her teeth when the sun shone, or after a good meal.

'Sated? In what respect?'

We laugh in tacit understanding. Not a word about anything like that. I was dead in the office too, and so I left both. Nobody had anything to say to anyone else. Not a thing. The rupture did us all good (and no doubt the others regretted it later).

So much for this session. When we parted Laurin said we would have to talk about authority. I dreamt about God in the night. But the next time we went back to the subject of wife and mother. Laurin wanted it this way. No doubt the fact that my wife was expecting a child had something to do with it. Sure, sure. But things of that sort are not of prime importance. The problem of authority goes much deeper. Laurin agrees with me. This time too, I counted out a hundred schillings in advance and put them on his desk as I left. Like the last time. Very discreet, very convenient. No accounts. I don't have to go to the post office. The money doesn't come between us. I admire Laurin's sensitivity!

But the second time I had to laugh as I walked through the courtyards to the street. It was almost like going to one of those awful women: fancy comparing Laurin to them! Isn't that funny? It shows what original ideas I can get!"

3

AT THIS point I would like to quote from the short report which Doctor Kralicek wrote for me:

"Judging by outward appearances the patient Zangl seemed healthy enough when he first came to see me. 33 years old, height about 1.78, well-fed, but certainly not fat. Admittedly the musculature was slack, particularly in the upper part of the body. His facial colour suggested a lack of fresh air. He struck me as a little nervous, his palms were damp, when he talked he occasionally showed a certain lack of concentration, but I thought he was definitely intelligent, perhaps a little above average. The only signs of abnormality were deep creases at the corners of his mouth, typical of people with stomach disorders. I carried out a physical examination and diagnosed a slight inflammation of the lower intestine, with a tendency to spasms. I immediately suspected the kind of mild disorder so common in a city practice. Not enough exercise, too heavy a diet, irregular hours and too much mental strain doing jobs that usually do not involve physical movement, so that not all parts of the body are exerted equally—all this leads to disturbed sleep and its accompanying symptoms.

I had absolutely no reason to suppose that there was any psychic abnormality. Most of my patients are old people who live on their own. Loneliness and financial difficulties often lead to physical and mental neglect, and in comparison the young man in question could be described as healthy. In addition his clothes gave no indication of instability. They were not, of course, very smart, but his coat and suit—albeit worn—were in good condition. Admittedly he could have done with a clean shirt and the heels of his shoes were trodden down, but bachelors who live on their own, and who are introverted and shy of social contact, often neglect their appearance, without one immediately diagnosing a deep depression or recommending a psychiatrist.

I naturally began by seeing if a medicine would help, and prescribed a suitable diet and a preparation which counteracts inflammation and cramps.

As I expected, purely pharmaceutical treatment was not totally successful. So I entered into a discussion on the patient's general circumstances. We medical practitioners often find that advice on the way patients lead their lives has more effect than automatic treatment with medicaments. I advised the patient at least to continue with his walks, perhaps to re-establish a physical balance by some kind of sporting activity. I pointed out that finding new human contacts would help his emotional stability. Sport, for example, might provide an opportunity for such contacts. It is only now, having seen his diary, that I know just how he misinterpreted my sensible advice. Nobody could accuse me of having advised him to seek contacts with prostitutes. I would like to emphasise yet again that I advised him to be more active, to have more social intercourse, to take more part in the world around him.

I did not have very many talks with him. I must admit that after a few sessions I did have the impression that this patient might be a complicated case, and that he should be referred to a specialist, but at this point the patient, who had at first been very co-operative, broke off contact with me, and I did not see him again, so that I had no opportunity to give him suitable advice. So far society has failed to give us doctors the legal means to treat patients against their own will, even when this would be for their own good."

So much for the picture from Dr. Kralicek's point of view. The dispassionate words of this no doubt honest and experienced general practitioner cannot quite conceal the fact that he believes himself unjustly reproached for the blunder of meddling in a therapy outside his scope, a blunder which borders on negligence. The feeling that he has been judged unfairly is revealed in the sarcastic little dig at a society which has given him inadequate legal means for dealing with cases of this kind.

I would like to permit myself a remark on this subject: society is to blame, but in a much more general way that Dr. Kralicek implies. It is not to blame with regard to the doctor, but is guilty in relation to the patient, having given him too little help in orientating himself, and allowing him to sink unheeded into his isolation, when this inadequate help broke down.

I am personally of the opinion that in Zangl we are concerned with a worthwhile personality, capable at times of really poetic insights beyond mere intellectual understanding.

But it is not the reporter's job to evaluate and accord blame. I would merely like to point out that Dr. Kralicek's account says nothing about consciously and deliberately undertaking psychoanalytic treatment, while the sick man's description leads one to suppose that the doctor was fully aware that this case extended into a sphere of medicine which his training did not qualify him to enter into. Clarity on this point must be established by the commission by a thorough interrogation of the doctor.

But let us allow the sick man to speak for himself at some length through his diary, in order to see the tragic inevitability with which he moved in a straight line towards his first murder.

"Today is *Sunday*. I can write all day! Last nights's dream has already been noted down. I did that while I was still at

home in bed. But I have now been alone with my Black Book
for many hours. I went to the library expressly for this. I
never take the BB away from its place. I'm hoping to catch
up with Laurin today. It's so complicated when one has to
make notes for the same day and simultaneously for another
day several days back. I might even begin to make notes on
writing about the same day and the one I am giving an
account of. No end to it! Like a hall of mirrors.

(I must avoid words like that: hotel, hall of mirrors—
filthy thoughts immediately come to mind and I start drawing and sketching plans again. But I want to write about
Laurin!)

I am at war with authority. I told Laurin quite frankly.
I don't tell him anything about the illicit third case. I
really couldn't say anything to Laurin about that. But
maybe I will one day—when he is familiar with my opinion
of God and knows what I think about good and evil. Otherwise he will think that is all there is to me, and I want him
to think highly of me. So I don't do anything illicit, but there
is a tense relationship all the same. I have to explain that in
more detail:

In the old days things were such that I was very small
and insignificant, while everything around me appeared to
be enormous and important. Teachers, dignitaries and
officials, people in uniform—all these people were not fallible
human beings to me, but symbols of their function. Because
I had no function, because I did not wear a uniform or fulfil
any office, I was afraid of them. I bowed and tried to ingra-
tiate myself with them. The fact that I shrank to such an
extent in their presence kindled a fierce hatred in me. Why
should I, of all people, be such a nobody? I tried to escape
from them, by going behind their backs. Even at school. Well,
later on it was all very different. It began with the plastics

king, I just cold-shouldered him. I know now that other people are weak and insignificant, even when they think that official authority gives them mastery over me. I am not afraid now. Ridiculous, to make such an assertion!

'Nobody is making such an assertion,' Laurin will say. Laurin, Laurin, he sees through me as though I were made of glass. I don't tell him that my final liberation was due to him. He has made the development in my life palpable. He has also changed me totally in other ways with his sympathetic advice. To give an example, the walk I took yesterday.

On Saturdays I close at lunchtime. So I went through very busy streets, Kärtnerstrasse, Graben. A lot of people, not like in the week. Then I saw one in green, wearing a woollen dress, with a gold chain round her waist, about twenty years old. She wore black lace gloves and carried a patent leather handbag. She walked along, looking into the posh, expensive shop windows at the goods displayed for the international public who come to our musical city, but she wasn't really looking at the furs and gold lamé dresses, but at the reflection of her face, which was also for sale. Not everybody is capable of such sensitive observations. I mean, can see allegories of that kind. All the same, I was not absolutely sure. She was not wearing stockings. They usually have stockings on. And it was an unusual time of day. But she was walking so slowly. She never looked at anyone on her other side. Always at the windows.

I was not sure. But then she slipped into the passage where they always hang about at nights. She was looking at rolls of cloth.

Suddenly—and it was just this that Laurin has changed— I thought: Speak to her! Verify reality!

But the lights were red, and I had to wait. God knows I don't want to get involved with the police, particularly on one of my walks. So I waited. I looked at her like a tiger at an unsuspecting roe. I was so certain. No violent thudding of the heart. For a moment I thought gratefully of Laurin.

But then nothing came of it after all, because an old libertine was suddenly standing just behind her. He was much shorter, and she had to stoop to hear his proposition. It only took a few seconds. Then he slipped away. She slipped after him. Now and again he glanced casually behind him, to make sure she was following him. I remember thinking: You beasts, don't think that I haven't seen through you! Then they disappeared into the narrow alley where the hotel is.

Although for the first time I was prepared to speak to one, I was quite glad that she had been snapped up under my nose. It would have been a shame about the money.

I went on walking for a long time, but saw nothing else. I knew perfectly well where I could have met someone else. But I didn't want to go to the Café Rabe. All those passers-by, and most of them know very well what goes on there! I'm not that blatant. I really don't understand these men who hang around certain street corners in the evenings, looking, and everybody knows why and what they are looking at. I, on the other hand, always walk past very fast, only looking out of the corner of my eye. Because that's quite normal. And Laurin says walking is very healthy. (I said to him a little while ago, running away from a painful desire to confess: I do such a lot of walking! But he's got no objection, so why should I upset myself about it?)

I don't want to wallow unnecessarily in these unpleasant matters. It is a good thing that I can think ahead now. Writing is thinking—and I can prepare for my next session with Laurin. Then the talk flows more easily, I get more into my hour. I would like to enthral him so much that he forgets the clock just for once. To the subject of wife and mother should be added, that the mother not only gives life, but also takes it away. Hence Mother Earth. Mother takes my life away. One can look upon mothers as givers, but also as takers. To me she seems more like a taker, if I am frank about it. And Laurin makes me completely frank. That's what is so marvellous about it. Suddenly I know so much. That was also why I left Constanze in the lurch: because she acquired a full belly. I simply could not stand it any longer. I struck her too, though I didn't say anything to Laurin about that. He must not get that sort of impression of me. Or only when he really knows my good side, the way I think about God. My lofty, spiritual portrait must be painted first, then I can reveal my inferior flesh.

I am quite intoxicated. Everything rushes in on me: thoughts, ideas. (The one in green, for example: perhaps I shall meet her later, when I go for my walk. I would soon show her, the moment we got to her room, that I am no ordinary customer. She must not think I am like that old chap yesterday. I could talk to her: perhaps she'll get fond of me . . .)

Monday

The eighteenth day of my acquaintance with Laurin, my seventh visit to the rose garden. How well prepared I was on authority! I laid it all out at his feet, beautifully clear and organised. He was very surprised. I think he was extremely astonished at my intelligence. Then we talked about the dreams for the first time. Originally he wanted to go on talking about my superiors, the people under whose authority I had come so far in my life, but I said this was of no importance. I was so anxious to get to the dreams at long last. He let me take the initiative. I told him of my attempt to tear down the villa by the sea. This reveals my relationship to the alleged highest authority: God.

Since there is no God—in the dream I expressed this through the quicksand, on which the house stands—I could use the current to undermine the foundations. But then the question arose : how could I direct the current?

The current is both : life and ordered rhythm, death and chaos. The villa is the structure of the individual life. These narrow shackles must be cracked. It would be convenient to utilise the current for this. But there is only sand : so how can I divert it?

A stranger shows me his factory, which also stands entirely on quicksand. An old cellar door beside the stamping machines leads to the grotto of Mithras. Down there is the sanctuary of a god of nature and of orgies. (By the way, it was only yesterday that I read in the paper about the orgies in Carinthia. Everybody seems to have orgies nowadays. I shall have more to say about papers later on.) But the door was barred.

'And there aren't any rocks?' asked Laurin.

Of course there are no rocks in a godless world !

But his remark shows how wise he is, how quickly he feels at home with strange ideas.

Then he talked a bit about the God of mercy and understanding. Asked me if I was an atheist. I had said so much as a matter of course 'since there is no God'.

No, I am not an atheist. It's just that for me HE does not exist. That's all. I don't resist ideas which don't exist for me.

Then Laurin said something very extraordinary. What worried him most was my trying to tear the villa down ! Why didn't I try to strengthen its foundations?

A question which completely took me by surprise. That had not occurred to me at all. But I am unable to give a sincere reply, I just say : 'You won't be able to talk me into your God !' For the moment I could say no more. I had not prepared for this. So I stammered something about 'order and freedom'.

I think the beach ought to be cleared of these useless buildings. They impede the waves and constrict one's sweeping vision. I detest pretty landscapes, green trees, houses. On the other hand I love the sea and wide stretches of sand. If I had a garden I would lay out the whole of it with the finest of white sand. I would keep on making it smoother and smoother. Cleaner and cleaner.

Laurin said nothing for a long time and propped his head on his hand. 'You worry me!' he said at last. 'We must try and make quicker progress.'

A remark like that really made me feel proud. A clever and important person was worried about me! He takes me so seriously that he ponders and considers. But I reassure him. I feel quite well, I said.

(The stool test last Friday was our last 'medical' theme: nothing organic indicated. Since then we have only talked about lofty matters, philosophy and ideas.)

What philosophers have I read, Laurin wants to know. But I can't think of anything for the moment. And psycho-analysis? Heaven forbid, no, I don't want anything to do with that sort of thing. Tracing everything back to filthy stuff, that meant turning one's back on the spirit!

Laurin said only: 'Really?'

Every person, he explained to me, had certain aggressive drives. He thought for a long time, whilst I allowed myself a little reminiscent digression to the one in green. (His searching look: could he read my thoughts? I hope not. I would be upset if he knew that I was not always concentrating on the matter in hand. The one in green is a long way from aggressive drives, since all I want to do is to gain her attention.)

Aggressive drives: one works them off in one's job and with the people one lives with. Had I thought of shutting down the library again? The devil I will. (Laurin always succeeds in getting me thoroughly worked up.) Just now of all times, when I have such important things to think and write about! A day is scarcely long enough to write down everything that goes through my head during that one day.

'Do you want to write instead of living?'

'Surely books are life? The written word represents the highest form of life!'

'But one can't write and live at the same time. There's a time for everything.'

'I do live. Running a library is something, surely?'

'You're right there.'

I am so proud when Laurin admits that I am right. Of course he does not know how little I actually do there. Particularly just now, during the last days of the month, with everybody going swimming, there is little demand for books. Most customers come because of the third case. What do I mean, most of them? All of them. What does all of them mean? There are only two or three a week. It's a good thing I can ask what I want of them. How could I pay Laurin otherwise? So I take their money and send them packing. One furtive youth I actually sent away empty-handed. He didn't dare to come out with what he wanted, and I didn't meet him half-way. I found him too repulsive. This musty torpor! Bad thoughts surrounded him like a cloud of bats, whilst I was thinking about God!

'What did the machines in the factory yard signify?' Laurin suddenly asked me.

I gave him an all-embracing answer. In fact they have a lot to do with the third case, about which he knows nothing. So I did not say anything precise. He was on my tracks right away, intelligent as he is. Just said: 'Lots of things. They have several meanings. Superficially something sexual, but actually the striving for order and harmony. Because there is nothing without sex.' Laurin laughed, and I felt good. (It's nice to make someone laugh.)

'Hardly a symbol without sexual connotations.' (Again he admits that I am right!) 'Because that's what we see in it.'

Watch it, that last sentence gave me food for thought. We are like a couple of tennis players. One shot leads to another.

'That's the main problem,' I said. 'One never knows what really is—and what we just imagine.' For instance, it makes me think of the city. I cut through a large chunk of it on my walk. It's full of whores! Wherever you go, these poisonous colonies of toadstools are everywhere, at every street corner. It's as though the town had only been built to provide corners for this foul fungus to settle on. It glitters and whispers and tiptoes and rustles in the darkness. Cigarettes glow in the dark, patent leather handbags gleam in the lights of passing cars. Sometimes it reminds me of the relay station of a telegraph office: contacts are established and broken, sorry, wrong number.

One ought to have a scythe, to crop this dangerous and poisonous form of life. But it would at once start sprouting again. Like fungus on rotting wood.

The whole city is like that. After all, I am only a product of it. It is the city's fault that I am like this. And yet people would point at me if I said it out loud.

My third case—that is my profane share of living humanity. The fact that I know this is what makes me special. The only question is: could I overlook the fungus and only pay attention to those houses in which people merely sleep? It is simply a matter of what one perceives. And Laurin understands all this, without any need for discussion. One single sentence from him replaces endless explanations which I would have had to give someone else. He is a genius, and I am his equal!

During a pause when I stopped writing I realised what a marvellous thing such a diary is. Not like a novel, which is artificial and thought out. In a diary life writes itself. It looks through my eyes and takes shape in my understanding, but it is genuine, what it says in my book. And it is so necessary! Because only a thought which has been written down is of value—the other goes under in the maelstrom of time and place. For example, if I had started keeping a BB earlier on, I would not have lost sight of whole areas, whole stages of my life. Nowadays I really only know what exists since I took over this library. What has happened since I really found myself. Since I have started living only for myself.

Since I gave up my conscience, in order to gain a soul! Because I have no conscience. How happy it makes me, to be able to say that. My third case—what I do when I get back home from my walk—what I draw and dream—what I intend to do with my technical apparatus—I say yes, happily! This is also part of the release I experienced when I left Constanze. At last I can be myself!

I do chatter on so!

I lie in my room and think with concentration. But to write it down—what an effort. My pencil can hardly keep up. Cannot keep up! So the BB is incomplete too! Laurin did say to me, when I told him about the way my thoughts flitted about and my inability to concentrate, that more contact with reality would help me. I will think about this during my walk and look for contact.

Tuesday

I have to tell myself to take things in their right order. There is so much to write down. It is like an avalanche, that keeps growing larger and larger. Like an approaching flood from which I can only escape by drinking it up. I drink by writing. To begin with last night: how obscene the word 'hotel' can be, when it glows in a narrow alleyway in the second precinct on a dark red luminous sign which sticks out of a wall like a chopped-off phallus! The street is dark.

Rubbish lies in the gutter. I thought I saw the one in green there! She was just going into the hotel as I turned into the alley. My heart beat like mad, although I had often come this way during my walks. No doubt it was because I had thought a lot about the one in green. My little microphones, which I had made up as hair slides, combs, brooches—during the past few days I had fastened them surreptitiously on her. (Only in thought, of course.) And it was for this hotel that I had made the remote-control cameras and tape recorders. I had also played with the idea of getting myself a job as a night porter here. My cubby hole the central control for a whole television network. I would have handed out roles to the guests like a theatrical manager. But I did not find the one in green when I went into the espresso bar next to the hotel entrance. That's what happens when you take the advice of a third person. For I would never have come here if it had not been for Laurin. He alone had brought it about, by saying: 'More contact with reality!'

Reality is always disappointing. A dimly lit room, full of nooks and corners. At the counter three men with fat backs. An old trollop at a small table. Her black-toothed smile is repulsive to me. I let her know it!

In an alcove three lads with their female companions. They are drinking beer. I am being stared at with bold impudence. I order a Turkish coffee. It has only just arrived when I hear the way the three in the corner are carrying on. The most obvious obscenities. Even I, who am totally unprejudiced, modern and uninhibited, cannot repeat them. Finally I say out loud—with my heart in my mouth— 'Gentlemen, if you must indulge in such filthy talk, kindly keep your voices down!'

The three look at me blankly, their female companions laugh shrilly, and the three men at the counter roar out: 'Not a bit of it, turn it up!'

The thick-set manager comes out from behind the bar and

walks over to the alcove: 'Keep your voices down, chaps! Just wait till the gentleman's left.'

What a cheek. I pay and leave without drinking the coffee. I don't care two hoots for this sort of reality. I heard them laugh impudently behind my back as I left.

I lay awake for a long time. The wind moaned in the chimney stacks and the airshafts of the house. A hatch banged rhythmically. At last I sank into the sea of sleep. The voices stretched out arms towards me and caught hold of me.

Then came the dream!

I dreamt about a temple in the middle of a rose garden. It was quiet and peaceful all around, after I had climbed over a dangerous chaos of rocks full of crevices. As I got nearer to the temple I was seized by a great excitement. It occurred to me that I had been searching after a secret for ages. Now I seemed to be near it. I slipped past a sleeping watchman, into the interior. A large, meditating Buddha sat in a hall filled with magic light. It was Laurin! I wanted to ask him to elucidate the secret, but he did not hear me. Because however hard I tried I could not utter a sound, I was stiff and lifeless too, and could not move. I woke up bathed in sweat. Outside the night was still stormy, and my window rattled.

Laurin asked me what I knew about Eastern mysticism, after I told him about the dream. But he was not satisfied. My yoga was profane. But I was flattered all the same. I did not know much about Zen. I would like to try it some time. After that you're supposed to be able to score a bull's eye every time. But Hesse made a deep impression on me. I read him just after the war. If I could only remember the title— it was a book about childhood, school and sexual awakening. But very lofty and worthwhile, although it had a title that had something or other to do with 'stupid'.

'Why Buddha?' asked Laurin.

I immediately explored the concept but all I could think of was brother-mother. Such a lot of nonsense. We both agreed that this time we had failed to get to the essentials right away.

I went on digging around mother, but failed to come up with anything. The only thing I kept on thinking of right away was the hotel where mother used to work. And the hotel in the Zirkusgasse. But I didn't want to say anything about that to Laurin. He doesn't know me well enough yet. Next time I must come better prepared, in order to be able to make a prompt diversion if we get near the dark. There was a real lull in the conversation. I found it embarrassing, because up till now we had always exchanged worthwhile and lofty thoughts. This time he must have thought me completely stupid. It was disillusioning, to see Laurin like this: a man who did not know how to go on. If it were not for the rose garden and the house with the many rooms which I do not know—I would be disillusioned. Yes, disillusioned. What a different person to the Laurin in my dream! But I must be more considerate. I always demand too much. No doubt his mind was somewhere else today. Some profound work he is just studying. Or something of that sort.

But then I got caught all the same. I was slow today, not at my best. It occurred to me during the most silent pause of the lull: the problem, for someone with profound thoughts on his mind, of living in a banal world. One is so high up that no echo is evoked anywhere. One is totally alone. Like mountain peaks. 'Everybody needs one or two people,' said Laurin. True, but it soon becomes a collective. Which is also why I avoid friendships. I love nature. The stormy tips of oak trees. Black forests full of profundity. The mountain heights. But I never go exploring. Wherever you go, you meet people. They ruin everything. Nobody is capable of such deep feeling as I am. I don't think anybody is.

People are the fly in the ointment.

'But one needs warmth!'

Sure, the collective offers shelter and warmth to everyone who submits to its narrowness. So stepping out into the wide open spaces of loneliness has to be paid for with considerable discomfort. But where is the greater greatness? In loneliness every time. Wagner, Beethoven, lonely heroes. Heroes do not grow in groups. I seek greatness.

Laurin does not laugh, looks seriously at me. For a long time. Then he asked: 'What is greatness?'

'Mastering life,' I said promptly.

Now I am nagged by doubts. Have I over-estimated Laurin? He did not seem able to follow me. Or did he fail to understand me because I was not on top of my form? (The experience in the coffee bar last night has confused me too much.) I am only too glad to learn. If I am to maintain contact with reality and if this excites me too much, I shall have to get used to reality. Perhaps I really do live too much on a spiritual plane. Just thoughts all the time. I ought to do things. (Play on words: I've been doing things with certain books for ages. I laugh at that.)

So I am a book-keeper of life: write down every smile. Only I have to measure it out in the correct doses so as not to drown in reality, so that I always remain able to keep a firm grip on it by writing.

This dream for instance: how much more important it is than all flat externals. A lofty dream.

I interrupted my writing a little while ago. I suddenly had a desire to live reality. I sat for a long time thinking worthwhile thoughts about human life. Unfortunately it has all slipped my mind. One ought to construct a machine which writes down thoughts without the effort that writing still involves. Thinking is so much smoother than speaking. How does a human being in fact think?

(A worthwhile question! I note it down, in order to work it out when I have a chance.)

Then I read the paper. Everybody reads the paper a different way. I, for example, start with the small ads. The personal column, there you see the true human face. For instance, it says: energetic amateur photographer seeks supple model. Replies to 'Daring Gallant'. A box number.

The advertisement starts me off on the most vivid thoughts for hours on end. Who could the amateur photographer be? Why energetic? Who would be attracted to 'energetic' in connection with photography? What would he photograph? And where? (I would love to put a little transmitter in his studio!)

I also compose letters. You have to wait and see what sort of answers you get. You throw the letters away, but might there be a few juicy photos with them? The wording just has to be daring enough, but then there's the problem of inserting the ad. I could never hand in words like that at the counter. I am much too sensitive for that.

Other ads too: ram seeks garden, in which he can be gardener. Or the 'open-minded married couple' who are always advertising for a 'like-minded' couple. What do they mean by 'like-minded'? Apart from the fact that they are open, I know nothing about their minds. Though I can imagine, if they put in ads like that.

Then it says in the paper: the young lad spied on the couple in the car and then shot them. That lad had real primitive courage! Like the judge, simply walking into the shop and saying: 'The third bookcase, please!' My predecessor started that procedure. The customers pass the formula on to each other. A small but faithful circle. They keep coming back. I could never do that! Which is one of the reasons I bought the business. I don't have to take the initiative. But I am already sick of it now. It bores me. What have I got for it, some books of photographs which are only worth looking at once. Actually it's a scandal, the way a good publisher can put something of this sort on the market quite openly. But it's like the emperor's clothes: nobody sees what he does see so long as he believes in something he doesn't see. Life is so terribly complicated.

Today I leafed through the Auschwitz book again: the most fantastic picture is the one with the Boger swing. And the other one with a whole mountain of corpses. All stark naked. They really were swine, those SS chaps. The things they saw! And the fellow with the whip! I'd like to catch the one in green like that! (Only I'd have to have a screen, so that she could not see me. But how could one use a whip from behind a screen? That's a technical problem I shall have to solve!)

Bold and tough. I'd like to have an Alsatian too. I'll buy myself some boots and a riding crop. I just tried it out with a ruler: a great feeling, when you hit it against your leg. It would be even better against leather. And then leather! Such a lot of people go riding nowadays. I bet it's because of that. They are just not as honest as I am, refuse to realise why they do things. The trouble with me is that I still have too little confidence in myself, in my knowledge of the basic motivations of the human soul. Or I would scream it into their faces. Things have improved because of Laurin. At least I can write now. Darkness. Time for my walk.

Wednesday

No dreams. Uneventful walk. Rain, and nobody in the streets. The bulbs must have burnt out at the hotel. The sign was not lit up. Ate beans with mayonnaise. Was sick. Could not sleep for ages.

Shall have to go and see Laurin later. What shall I tell him? It is gradually becoming uncanny. What does he know? And how? Writing is so difficult today. I've got nothing to say, that's what it is. But one can't always have something to say. One must have creative rests. Perhaps my amateur radio would help. I could invent an enormous fly-trap, for butterflies.

What shall I say to Laurin? I've spent the whole time inventing. But with success. How they'll stare! (Thought of a party for butterflies: one after another they go into the trap by the third case, which I shall wire for high tension electricity, so that they burn up like moths.)

Last time I saw him Laurin used a significant word. He said that my relationship to other people is twisted. I had admitted that I had no girl-friend at the moment.

'But you are a man,' he said, and I thought I saw him smile.

I laughed too.

But my conscience is troubling me. I said 'at the moment' —but in fact it is two years. Since I've had the library. That's what I've got it for, after all. Whatever you do is wrong: if you've got no one, you get nowhere; if you've got someone, you don't want to get anywhere. Instead of reading my books, I read my other books. That's how it is. A complicated situation. One time I wanted to read a book about Nordic runes. Never touched it again. So profound, these Nordic sayings, every word in the language hides a secret. Perhaps it was the wisdom of the ancients I wanted from Buddha. The temple seems to indicate that. I'll buy something for my nerves. After that I won't be so sleepy any more, but will work productively. Untiringly. I am only putting the raw material down here. Simply write everything down. I'm like a deep sea diver, who brings things up to the surface.

Later on he will examine it. Now he is collecting material. I shall surprise Laurin with a lecture on the human condition. It's like this: man is really alone. At bottom, I mean. Love is a mirage, a reflection, one sees that part of oneself in the other person that one cannot see directly. Who can see his backview without a mirror? Nobody. The love partner is a mirror.

Of course one does not love every mirror, only the one where one fits into the frame. Everyone has the friends he deserves.

I have said something very instructive there: friends! Relationships to friends are of prime importance. Much more important than to lovers. Because love is nothing but friendship enriched with sexuality. What is sexuality? It is the desire to do something forbidden. How boring. It is quite another matter with total strangers: to start with everything is forbidden, even lustful looks. Gradually you work your way closer, then you attack the thing. And you do what is forbidden. That's wonderful. Which is why love is all nonsense. It's simply that people generally are not as honest as I am. They don't want to admit to themselves that they want to do what is forbidden. That's why they call it love and put a halo round it. (Suddenly I'm under way again: I have found the thread. If it were not for Laurin—I would have a totally useless afternoon!)

I am sure there is nothing twisted about this attitude. I only need to explain it clearly to Laurin point by point:

that I don't look for friendship, because I know that it is only a mirage. I am my own friend, because I am honest and also know my hidden side: I reflect myself to myself,

that I regard love as doing what is forbidden. That I do not need it, because for me there is no such thing as something forbidden. I am strong and live honestly—I accept everything, do not need to suppress anything. Therefore do

not need love. I can deal with the urge simply enough.
Monks do too,
    that we must talk about the question of consciousness.

On the last point: a man 'knows' what he sees with his eyes,
but only a certain section. If he looks this way, he can't see the
other way. It's the same with knowledge: if I happen to be
thinking of the problem of God I can't worry about the radio
problem. That is my main problem: I want an all-embracing
harmony, in which I know and see everything. But a man
cannot do that. That is the fate of mankind. To talk in
biblical terms: the fact that mankind can only see, think,
know, feel in sections—that is the curse of man, the result
of original sin, the eviction from Paradise, where no one saw,
knew or thought anything. To float quietly in warm water!
To be a corpse floating feet first out of the cat hole twelve
metres below the surface! That's my idea of paradise.

    Now I must go. Today I have ammunition enough for
Laurin!

Have just come back. Had the following dialogue:
    'What you say is very interesting.'
    'I'm not saying it to be original. It's what I think!'
    'I didn't say original, I said interesting. There's a differ-
ence.'
    'You're right there. I apologise. But what did you mean?'
    'You're so fantastically remote.'
    'It took me a long time to get to them, believe me. It hasn't
been easy for me.'
    'I didn't mean remote from your problems. You're so
remote from them that you don't even see them any more.'
    'I don't have any problems.'
    'Why did you come here?'

'I don't know.'

'I'll tell you : because of stomach trouble.'

'Oh yes, so I did !'

(Laughter.)

'And why are we talking?'

'Because we enjoy it. Because it's good for our insides. Most of all, because it's interesting.'

'What is interesting?'

'My remoteness. That's what you just said. My remoteness from what?'

'From life, from human beings, from reality.'

'I'm an observer. I don't get involved.'

'Why not?'

'Because there is not sufficient reason. What should one get involved in? Everything is true. Everything is false. Everything is good. Everything is bad. In other words, it all depends on your point of view. How should I know what standpoint to adopt? I could adopt any standpoint. That's my many-sidedness !'

'That's your weakness.'

'Weakness? Why, may I ask? I call that strength !'

'Strength is like a tortoise shell. You are suffering from too much shell. Too much calcification. Why?'

'Shells are always for protection. If I should have a shell, as you maintain, it would be for my own protection.'

'Protection from what?'

'Well, from life, of course ! What else?'

I'm always amazed at Laurin's quick mind. Because I often think I've got the better of him. When he lets me take the lead. But then I find he's in front of me by a short head after all. But I always catch up with him. The question : 'Why do you have to protect yourself from life behind a shell?' was one I had asked myself before he did.

It is a good thing that he knows me so well. He is a frame into which I fit. He is my friend. I find my reflection in him.

On this occasion I particularly relished putting the money on the table for him. I could have drowned in that mirror.

What does that mean? What would this drowning be? It would be my suddenly thinking that my fault was not having any faults. That I longed to commit a fault. To do something forbidden, something that really is prohibited. Because Laurin secretly thinks—how clearly I see through him—that I should give up my existence as an exceptional human being, that I should climb down from my greatness to the narrowness below, should have faults like other people, who get hurt because they are so bad.

Perhaps I deceive myself about myself! Yes, I am honest enough to harbour this thought. Perhaps there is something forbidden to me, and I do not admit it to myself! For example, I did not go into the coffee bar where I thought I would meet the one in green. And I never look on my walks. Could this be because I think it wrong to look? I shall conduct an experiment! This evening, when I go for my walk, I shall do something which I am really not allowed to do!

Thursday

I went straight over to the Zirkusgasse after I had shut up shop. Usually I go through the town in loops and curves. I know a coffee bar in the Mariahilferstrasse, a wine and spirit shop on the Gaudenzdorfer Gürtel, where women of that sort hang about. There's a pub by the cathedral where they look like ladies. And they cost a lot there. They don't stand out there, but when I pass the window I recognise them all the same. Then my heart pounds.

The Zirkusgasse, on the other hand, is not ambiguous at all. It is clear and straightforward. The girls stand to left and right of the hotel entrance. Like a red, festering rash round an ugly mouth. The lit hotel entrance is the mouth. Three steps up. White light runs out like saliva. And the women all round. Like mushrooms. (In the public park, for instance, it's different yet again: there you get couples sitting on benches, and people out walking dogs on leads along the gravel paths. Some women wandering about in the dark are quite normal. Others aren't. You never know for sure. It's a muddle.)

It's all quite different in the Zirkusgasse. For me, to wander into it is like the drift of a fish. When I turn round the corner into this narrow street it's as though I was plunging into water. I float along, a silent stranger, under waving seaweeds. One in a red dress could be a coral reef. And my heart does not pound so hard here. 'It' is all right here. Because it stinks. And because it is shabby, dark and dirty. It is much warmer than the clean, well-lit café. The fish feels out of place there. A fish out of water. Weak and motionless. He is afraid to twitch his fins. When he encounters an inviting glance he looks the other way.

The Zirkusgasse is not light, mundane and groomed. Everything fits in: I, the surroundings—everything.

The girls don't just stand there. They stand for a bit, then they start walking slowly the other way. Then they stand again, like fish in a current. They sway up and down on high heels, their backsides rolling and swinging. Their arms swing languidly under the weight of the heavy patent leather bags. In these receptacles they carry the tools of their trade, like workmen. A whole labour force, like a lot of mechanics. Always at the ready. The tools of the trade are make-up and lipstick, rubber goods, a few worn photos for propaganda. Maybe a knife too? Right away, I was sure I would meet the one in green. I had thought about her so much! I took it as a matter of course when I saw her at the end of the line. I walked past the others and ignored their gestures, their whispers, their bright glances.

I had almost caught up with her when she turned round. But she did not recognise me. So my hand, which I had joyfully proffered, remained sticking out at waist level. So then I fished out a cigarette packet and pushed one into my mouth as I walked past.

At the same time she whispered, not directly to me but into the night air: 'Coming with me, darling?'

I saw the movement of mouth and jaw as she let the words float out like the breath one sees on a frosty winter morning. It was the movement of a charming but sick bird drinking.

I had heard this sentence whispered, murmured, breathed so many times. They all use it. It is like a ceremonial. Like actresses in an age-old play. Every movement, every breath is laid down by rule. Some acted it mechanically. The green one still does it with feeling. She lives her part.

I'm sure she expected me to walk past. When I stopped two paces away from her she turned round quite astonished. Our eyes met!

And Laurin says it's difficult for me to make contact! He should have seen that look! We really sized each other up! And immediately came to an understanding! Two strangers in the same boat after a disaster at sea. Under conditions of that sort people don't stand on ceremony, they just ask straight out: 'Have you got any food?'

'How much?'

'Seventy and the room.'

And she couldn't have been much over twenty. So cheap! She's throwing herself away, making herself too cheap. I almost told her so. And when she said it she looked at me so pleadingly, as though she was apologising about the money. She had a black eye, the one in green. I immediately felt so sorry for her I would have liked to have given her two hundred and caressed her eye.

'Okay.'

'Have you got a fag for me?'

I gave her one. No, I didn't want to start that way with her, coming empty-handed. I've known her for such a long time.

Not today. I'll come back tomorrow. Maybe she could come to my place. I suddenly feel shy about going into that hotel. Not because of people watching. Not because of the money. Simply: this hotel is the end. Rock bottom.

'Not today. Got no time.'

'Pity!'

She turns her head away. I'm sure she feels hurt. Trusted me and named her price and the hotel—and I turn her down! I was already sorry by the time I had walked one step away from her.

'Pity!' she had said. It was not because of the money that she was sorry, but because of me. She would like to have gone with me. Maybe even for nothing. I would only have had to pay for the room.

I turned back the moment I got to the end of the street. Now I'm going to take her with me, come what may! Although I almost ran someone else had already gone off with her. I just caught sight of her being sucked into the mouth of the hotel. An oily chap with a trenchcoat and a briefcase. I bet she charged him twice as much. And maybe she was thinking of me when she did it?

All the same, I was very glad. The experience had made me feel light-hearted and at ease. The world was my oyster. I almost went up to one of the others after all, to buy myself one, I suddenly felt so strong and sure of myself. But that's the funny thing: one doesn't need anything when one is strong and sure of oneself.

So I went home and thought about the one in green and about tomorrow and what it would be like.

The fact that she had asked so little on account of her black eye had touched me very much. Someone had hit her. No doubt he wanted to punish her. But no doubt, too, she was not agreeable to being punished. And yet she had accepted her punishment, in that she had lowered her price on account of the black eye. How can you hit someone as humble as that! I would not have hit her, if she had been as humble as that with me—no matter what she had done.

I'll take her something from the third case. A book of pictures. Just two girls together. I particularly go for that. And I'm sure she'll like it too. She gets the other thing all the time. And she will be pleased with it. It'll appeal to her, be to her taste, and I'll sit beside her and watch her pleasure. Then she can talk to me a bit: the way she lives and how she came to this profession. Who gave her the black eye. And I'll hold her hand while she's talking. Then she'll cry and put her head on my shoulder. I'll comfort her and whisper little things in her ear:

'There, there, don't cry, I'm here.'

Then I'll give her the money and she'll ask when I'm going to come again. Because I didn't want anything from her. She's never had a customer like that! Who only wants to see her happy and be nice to her for a bit.

I thought about all this until late last night, and this morning I lay in bed for a long time and thought about the one in green. She must have sensed it.

At the shop I also thought about her, as I selected the book and wrapped it up nicely. It's still in very good condition. I've almost never lent it out. So it really is something personal! In addition I put in a slip with the name of the shop stamped on it: a bit of me, yet anonymous all the same. I'm always very tactful. I was so busy with all this that I almost forgot to go to Laurin.

Laurin asked me why I was in such a good mood.

I said pertly: 'Aren't I allowed to be?'

Then he laughed good-humouredly and said he was pleased. That's what we were there for.

I apologised. But I too sometimes descend from the heights of philosophy.

Then he probed around for a bit: why was I in a good

mood, how often was I, how long since the last time, and why not up till now. But I couldn't explain it to him. It was a useless conversation. This time I was sorry about the hundred schillings at the end. Today I shall have my little hour of chat elsewhere. How stupid to call him Laurin! When he is only Dr. Kralicek. And the surroundings are really far from magical. Tenement blocks and just his small, overgrown garden.

I too would love to have a garden, because I love nature so much. And I don't even have a pot of chives!

If I get on well with the one in green she might help me with the other things. The business with the microphones would be much simpler with her help. I would merely have to sit in the cupboard. Providing it is large enough! That would be marvellous! I've got an appetite for deeds now. No more just sitting and thinking. Shake off the dust. I really must sort things out in the library. I could make things for the one in green. I've had enough experience with synthetic materials! I would do it for her for nothing at all. My reward would be the joy of being able to do something for her. And maybe we would move in together. And then she would always tell me everything. And perhaps she would bring home a girl-friend now and then. These girls always have girl-friends! And then I could rescue her from the mire in which she is stuck. She would be very grateful to me on that account. And would do anything I wanted! I'm sure her name is Christa. I just know. I'm such an intuitive person.

Friday

And when all I wanted was to be good to her! What scum! Well, she paid for it. But one thing at a time. Nobody has ever disappointed me so much. I must remain calm.

First I went home. After work. I washed, and put some perfume on. The new suit. A handkerchief in my breast pocket. I didn't want to eat anything. All the same, I did not want to get there too early. I kept on thinking about what I should say. Get things on a personal level from the start. Be jolly, but not cheeky. Friendship has to be built up and cultivated, one has to give up all of oneself and go along with the other person. Then you win their heart!

Not with one of those though! I've learnt that now. I got there at about nine. With the book under my arm. I was happy and excited. Said hullo to the others. After all, they are colleagues of my one in green. I could give a party for them all. Maybe when the green one has her birthday. (I didn't think of the butterfly trap at that moment. I was really feeling very amiable and affectionate, didn't want to burn anyone up in a blue flash.)

But she was not there. That was the first disappointment. I went up and down the alley four times. Nothing in green.

Then she suddenly gets out of a car. It had been standing by the dark kerb all along. She must have seen me. And yet she went on sitting there. A brutal type, that man. With thick arms and a fat head. A Mercedes-Diesel of course—the same types always drive the same cars. She waved to him, with a languid movement of her left hand, from the hip, while she swayed over to the entrance of the hotel. I stand in a dark doorway and watch her. She is not wearing the green one, but a blue one.

Today of all days. I wanted to throw the book away and go.

I would have spared myself a good deal if I had done just that.

Then she moved away from the three girls who were standing there and came towards me. I also move away from the doorway and walk towards her. Like clockwork. The figures are moved closer together by a concealed mechanism. My mind was a blank at that moment. My hands were quite dry, my pulse steady. Only my eyes burned. They protruded like periscopes, into so-called reality. I sat in my HQ, in warmth and quiet. I ordered: 'Fire!'

'I have got time today.'

'Time for me, darling?'

'Sure.'

'Hundred and fifty and the room.'

'A hundred and fifty?'

'. . . and the room.'

'But why? It was only seventy yesterday.'

'Yesterday? Were you with me yesterday?'

'Don't you even know?'

'Could be. But that was before nine. After that it's a hundred and fifty.'

'Get away! When I've been back home on purpose to spruce myself up for you. I've thought a lot about you . . .'

'Well, what do you want to do? Suit yourself, darling. If you don't fancy it—there's others.'

'Wait a minute.'

'Are you coming?'

'Yes. All right.'

'Well, let's go then.'

I was like a stone. I simply was not there. As though pulled along. Her half a yard in front. Suddenly fast, no more slinking, no rolling backside. Now she is throwing her hips forward and marching straight into the trap with me behind. Not to the right. Not to the left. Two girls at the entrance step aside. Smoking, not looking. The one in blue leads me up two steps, across the coconut matting, five paces, the porter. He squats in his niche. An old man with no teeth. He wears a large, crudely mended pullover. Unshaven. Mummy's hotel was different. This is no hotel.

(In mummy's hotel I was never allowed in the entrance hall when I visited her, I had to use the entrance in the courtyard, where the dustbins stood, overflowing with refuse from the kitchen. The corridors like those here with blister-

ing walls and an unpleasant smell, for the staff. But there
the hotel also had hallways and staircases carpeted in red,
apart from the back stairs of grey concrete, which I had to
use. Iron doors stood between the two worlds. Here there
are no iron doors to a better world. This world is the whole,
round, entire world.

'Thirty for the room.'

I gave the old man fifty. Such a poor old fellow! The one
in blue had already gone on ahead with the key in her hand.
She stopped on the stairs and looked back. I did not look at
her. Such a narrow staircase. A winding one. Half-way up
we come to a halt: traffic the other way. But at first I don't
look. And then I do, but search in vain for signs on their
faces. A banal, grey, commonplace face, totally vacant. Now
it grins confidentially. I could spit. The woman, on the other
hand, has a matter-of-fact expression. She could be on the
stairs of a government office.

'Come on then.'

The steps hang crooked out of the wall. One could fall.
Keep going, the blue-green one keeps going on up the stairs.
On the second floor a narrow passage on the left. Also
crooked. Laid with linoleum, large patches of it missing. The
sound of running water behind a door. The key turns in the
lock with a tinny sound. The door is thin, no massive wood,
the lock loose.

Light.

I should have brought some flowers. And something to
drink. The room is small. Dirty grey wallpaper, two windows
with brown, peeling frames. Flowered curtains, crooked, the
linen faded, almost too small to cover the windows. A wide
bed, oak, massive, age-old, black. Little table with a marble
top. A cigarette end on the floor. A wash-basin, but no towel.
A greasy, lopsided armchair. The stuffing hanging out of the
arms and at the edge of the seat. Like hair out of the ears
and noses of old men. I lock the door.

'How d'you want it? It's two hundred without.'

'Here, a present.'

'What for? It's money I want.'

I stand by the door, at a loss, looking at her.

She's different after all. You can't really see it out in the street. Older, her skin not as smooth as I thought. The colour of white flour. Her slack mouth bright red over blackish teeth. At least thirty, looked at in the light.

Is she in fact my one in green?

She still has the black eye. It is green today. Changed colour, like the dress. But who cares, I've got to . . .

'A book? What rubbish!'

She has unwrapped it and placed it on the table.

'Do I get my money?'

'Of course!'

'Well, what do you want then?'

'Well, just to chat a bit.'

'Two hundred and fifty. But you can have an hour for that."

'Is the time important?'

'No, sweetie. We'll see.'

'Have a look at it.' I pointed to the book.

'The present first, darling.'

'You mustn't ask for presents. I'll give it to you.'

She picked up the book, opened it, giggled.

'What a lovely dirty book. You like things like that then?'

'Do you like it?'

'It's okay. But what about the present? That comes first.'

'But you've already had one.'

'Thanks a lot. But I mean my money.'

'Maybe you're avaricious?'

'Come off it, darling. You get nothing for nothing.'

'The book—do you know how much it is worth?'

'Okay, okay. It's a lovely book. But am I supposed to eat off it? Got to pay the hairdresser and the rent and the hire purchase—why am I telling you all this? It just spoils the atmosphere. Don't stand about like that, sweetie, give me the money.'

'I like hearing about you. Your personal affairs. Where do you live?'

'I live where I live, don't you worry your head about that. And my personal affairs—we'll talk about them another time.'

'D'you have someone to love?'

'Why are you asking so many questions? Are we going to bed or aren't we? I've got to watch the time!'

'I mean well. I'm not interested in bed. How you live, why you're in this job, the way you feel.'

'I'll tell you everything, darling, only I want the money first. Two hundred and fifty for a full hour. Or maybe you want a speciality job? D'you like getting beaten? Or master and slave? That costs four hundred.'

'No, nothing like that. You don't take me for a pervert, do you?'

'Well, darling, that's enough now. Are you going to give me my present or not?'

'There!'

I gave her the money. All of five hundred. I would have given it to her afterwards, even if it had only been seventy. It is all so terribly disillusioning.

'Get undressed then, darling.'

'What for?'

'Well, all right. Shall I? D'you fancy a bit of looking?'

'Oh yes.'

She starts getting undressed. The blue dress is carefully slipped down over her shoulders. She is careful about her hairdo. But it's quite different from what I imagined. She is so far away, so cold and businesslike. I miss her joy. It was her duty to enjoy it a bit. What was I paying so much money for? It's already five hundred and fifty with the room.

I'm just not made for girls like her. I'm not nearly enough
of an egoist for that. Her other customers—for them what
she feels is a matter of indifference. But for me it's not a
question of what I feel, but only what she does. She should
have a beautiful hour.

'And now?'

She stands in front of me in her black underwear. Noisily
sucks spit out of a dental cavity.

'What are you thinking about?'

'What am I supposed to think about?'

'Aren't you thinking about the book?'

'Come off it! Stuff like that has never got me excited yet.
Or shall I look at it now?'

'You do what you want. I only want your enjoyment.'

'All right, I'll read some.'

She lies down on the bed and reads. I watch her. Wait.

'I quite forgot: what's your name, darling?'

'Peter.'

I lie, because I don't want to commit myself totally. Since
I already feel that it is not going to turn out the way I
thought. (It's a good thing I didn't write my name on the
slip of paper.)

'My name's Evelyn.'

She turns the pages in a bored fashion. Wets her finger
with spittle.

'Got a fag?'

'Of course. Here you are.'

'Thanks.'

She gives me a searching look, from head to foot. Smiles.
I stand before her, give her a light. Is there something wrong
with my clothes?

'Am I doing it all right?'

'Well, yes. You're supposed to like it.'

'What do you want then? I'm doing everything you tell
me to do.'

'Will you come and see me some time?'

'Maybe . . .'

'I've got some more books like that.'

'You're a sly one, aren't you?'

'I suppose you think I'm funny?'

'No, I don't. You're not the only one. There's some I've only got to tell things to and they come.'

'What?'

Suddenly my heart beats like mad.

'Shall I? But then you'll have to give me some more—fifty.'

'I'm not a pervert.'

'Well then, get undressed and come over here.'

But I don't want to. How can I win her? I'm ready to give her anything, if only she would love me a little. I'd be wax in her hands. If, out of love, she would let me whip her a little, very gently, only so it makes a bit of a smacking noise. I'd put on boots. But she would have to beg me: 'Whip me, my sweet!'

'Well, darling, the hour's up.'

She shuts the book and stands up. I hadn't looked at the clock. Was the hour really up so soon?

'And you, Evelyn—did you enjoy it?'

'Sure I did! Marvellous! And it was so easy. I could have an easy life if all the fellows were like you.'

'Really?'

'Sure!'

'Shall I come again?'

'Any time! You can come any time.'

'Do you really like me?'

'Well, why shouldn't I?'

'How do I know that I can believe that?'

'All right, don't believe it then.'

She puts her clothes back on.

'But I'd like to believe it. You see, that's the way I am. I only think of you. Maybe you'd like to give me a present?'

'Me give you something? What shall I give you?'

'Anything. A stocking, maybe?'

'You're welcome. I've got a torn one. Can you replace it? A pair like that is expensive. Sixty schillings, you know!'

'I only want one. Will you give it to me for fifty?'

'Only 'cos it's you.'

After that I went to the station buffet. My stomach felt quite weak. My hand shook as I drank the beer. The taxi drivers and news-vendors looked at me oddly. I had not behaved like a man : taken the woman and finish. But I don't want to be like that. I am not brutal! I want to be kind and tender. To be a good human being! Whilst I spooned away at the goulash soup I again went over the whole thing step by step. I don't care about her name not being Christa. But that I had to give her the money first—and then, in fact, get nothing for it! And it came to six hundred altogether. An expensive torn stocking. I surreptitiously pulled it out of my pocket, rolled in a ball, when no one was looking, and sniffed it. No perfume even!

I've done it all wrong. On the one hand I gave way too much, on the other hand I was like a block of wood. Not a bit relaxed and cheerful. I should have made her laugh. That's it. Suddenly I know what I did wrong. If she had just once been gay and at ease. The way old friends are together.

For one thing is clear to me : we never stopped being formal with each other. The way it always is with a conscience. But I haven't got one. I am me. I should have made that clear to her. I was not in a position to do so. Just a bit different, and everything would have been fine.

She might have enjoyed it. But that way it was only work for her. And for me?

If only I could give up wanting to be a good person. Why do I consider her so much? It only makes me happy to see her happy. A pity about the book. It won't make her heart beat any faster. Maybe she'll sell it to the next one she sees.

I paid a thousand for it. Fifteen first-class photos. And so beautifully bound. A real collector's item. So all in all, one thousand six hundred. Was she laughing at me now? This thought makes me quite ill. Being used like a fool. And her friends will laugh out loud when she tells them. Filthy whores! But it's not like that. She said that it was nice. None of the others are so personal about it. Maybe she's thinking about me. And she said I should come back. Heartfelt assurances are not their style. Perhaps she really meant it. Then she loves me, in her own fashion. My fashion is different too. I don't think badly of her anyway.

If only I knew whether she thought badly of me? After the third beer I find a very simple solution: I'll go and ask her. Only I'll have to ask her in a cunning way, so that she can't lead me by the nose.

Three houses before the hotel is a used car lot. A ruined old dump. A wire-mesh fence in front of it. Floodlights shine on the cars, but they are switched off at midnight. It is now ten past.

I stopped there, pushed back the fence, it was possible to get through. Not even a watch dog. The girls keep walking up and down in the light. Do they still come past after twelve? I wait. Don't even dare to smoke. Nobody must see me. In which case they might point at me and laugh: there's Evelyn's suitor!

And she really does come! I can't grasp it. So she really does love me. My longing has drawn her here.

'Evelyn!'

I whispered through the wiremesh. She does not hear me. 'Evelyn!'

She hears me, stops, tries to make out my figure.

'It's me: Peter!'

'Who?'

'The one with the book. I've just been with you.'

But she was not as delighted as I thought she would be. She stopped where she was, came no closer.

'What d'you want?'

'To make love. Really, this time.'

'Why don't you come out of there?'

'I can't. I've got something to tell you.'

At last she comes nearer.

'I've got no more money, you know.'

'No money, no love!'

'Just a quick one.'

'Where? In there? It costs thirty in a car. But ten, since it's you. Have you still got that much?'

'Sure. Just come here. I've got to ask you something!'

She really does come in. She trusts me!

'Have you had another customer?'

'Is *that* what you want to ask me?'

'No. Where have you got the book?'

'Where's the twenty? I don't spend a lot of time hanging about in the street, you know.'

'I wanted to ask you something quite different . . .'

'Well, what is it?'

'You've already had enough money from me, haven't you? You'll get it, all right.' My hands are quite damp. I wipe them on the stocking. Otherwise I would really have had no reason to pull it out.

'You greedy shit! I'm not hanging round here any longer . . .'

She wanted to go. I tried to hold her back. My question was so important, but how can I ask carefully, if she doesn't want to hear? It wasn't a question of the money. I'd gladly have given her the twenty. But I didn't want to stand there like a fool again. That I had sworn to myself. How could she love me if she didn't pay any attention to me?

But she twists away, calls out: 'Let go of me, you filthy brute!'

I try to hold her mouth shut. She kicks into my shin.

At that point I suddenly saw red!

The stocking round her neck, tighter and tighter, I only wanted her to shut up, I damn well had a right to ask the question, anyone who doesn't want to hear can suffocate, tighter and tighter, until there is peace, the body twists, scratches and bites, that hurts, pull harder and press, I'll show you, you'll shut your trap, I tell you, go on, open your mouth wide, your filthy mouth, no more air for you, I'll show you who's boss. Well, so you're still at last. She lies on the ground, between my legs, quite close to the street. I pick her up by the shoulders and drag her behind the row of cars. She does not move.

'Evelyn?'

But she does not whisper back. Just the click-clack of high heels in the street.

In her ear: 'Evelyn: do you love me?'

No answer.

I take her bag and put it under her head. I fold her hands on her body. A good thing it's dark. I can't see her face. Perhaps it's a bluish red. Green, blue, blue-green, blue-red. Red. Dead.

That's the whole story.

Saturday

That was a refreshing sleep! I feel fine. All the same, I managed to keep going and write it all down in one go. Straight afterwards. I was really worked up, a marvellous feeling of animation. And I think I did rather well. The language seems powerful, the images vivid. I should always be able to write in this pointilliste fashion. And of course I was drawing freely on rich resources. What an experience! For only the doer has knowledge. To that extent Laurin is right.

I took a bath and had an ample breakfast. It is already three. I really slept like a stone. I think it was five when the light in my room went out. At any rate the first of the early workmen were already out on the street. Had an unbelievably vivid dream.

I'm glad I don't have to go to Laurin today. It is Saturday today. I've got things to do. Must take some notes before the colours fade. One forgets so easily. Now for example: the thud of the balls from the tennis court over there, people walking under the trees. The pulse of life goes on. That's the difference with literature: one can write 'The End'. But this goes on. In a little while I shall only have theoretical memories. Then one point follows the next. Now I still feel everything. How I would like to tell Laurin about it, tell him that I am a different person! That I'm a doer, not a dreamer!

But he might misunderstand me. I would have to take him there and show him the body. (If it were bloodier, it would be more impressive! A remnant of dissatisfaction remains. I was not totally adequate.)

The whole of life is like my relationship to the one in green: every act just a symbolic gesture, more or less. Every person nothing but a symbol for others. What symbol was the one in green for me?

I think she was a lot of symbols, all enclosed in one apparition. How does Goethe put it? 'All transitory things are only a likeness!' How true those words suddenly seem! As I have already said: Only the doer has knowledge. The one in green was a mirror for me. That is why I loved her. I found my reflection in her, but I spat into the mirror, with stone-hard saliva. The mirror broke.

Now she is nothing to me but a bundle behind a row of cars. The hotel is nothing but a shabby box. I don't understand the people who go there. I don't need it any more. Now I know it. The call of unlived life was what prompted my walks. Now I have lived it. (Nothing about it in the papers yet. The car dealer must have opened his eyes wide this morning!)

I sometimes ask myself whether I feel sorry for the one in green. But although I look into myself quite impartially, let all my feelings speak, all those that make themselves heard in any way at all: I am not sorry about anything. If she had shown me a little bit of love, she would have got off lightly. But I am glad she didn't. What would have happened? She would have sat round in my library, poked about in the third case, got me excited, so that I wouldn't have been able to think or write any more. Perhaps she would have dragged some of her women friends round, forced me to give parties. I would have sunk completely in that mire. But this way I have freed myself. Through a manly deed. The very fact that it was unpremeditated is what makes it manly: to grasp instinctively at what is right—and wham! So my blood speaks after all, when it comes to it. And toughness wins.

And the piece of humanity that I sacrificed was not worth much. It bore no relationship to what I shall achieve now. I feel an inexhaustible creative energy in myself. Write, write! It was worth it for that. Every man has a right to happiness —and my happiness is to create. Whatever stands in my way must go. That is the price of genius, that it must demand victims. I now bear the burden of being a murderer. But I bear it with head held high. In other ages I would have been borne shoulder-high through the streets: the hero, who slew the slimy dragon. In our slimy age I stand opposed to everything which represents dragon's teeth. And everything is the dragon's tooth. Only Laurin and me. (Oh, if only I could talk to Laurin about that!)

But how to tell him? Shall I tell him, if she had just shown love?

What is love? Something different for the one in green than for Laurin, undoubtedly. And something very different for me!

Or shall I say that I am proud to bear the burden of being a murderer?

Murderer! What sort of a word is that—it has no meaning for me, and if it had one, it would be quite different from that of the penal code.

Proud, what does proud mean?

What is the dragon?

No, nobody will understand.

How imprisoned one is in language! It only consists of yes-yes and no-no. One can never say what really is. The clarity of speech is its own death. And yet it is only clarity which makes it comprehensible. It is there for comprehension. What is comprehension? Expressing essentials. And essentials are essentially obscure. Language reminds me of the machine for blowing out matches: dreadfully pointless—and yet one cannot live without it. At least I cannot live without a machine for blowing out matches!"

4

IN THE middle of his daily entries Xaver Zangl breaks off his preoccupation with reality and returns to the philosophic speculations which seem more real to him than any reality. For reality is chaos to him, a chaos in which he drowns. The streets of Vienna, the houses full of people, the daily life all round him—he does not take it in, does not want to take it in, because (so he thinks) it would make too many demands on his powers of perception, and stop him from concentrating wholly on his search for the system whereby the moments of the day could be put together in a personal record. The flippant way Zangl says that he could not live without a machine for blowing out matches cannot disguise the pain he feels at the lack of a convincing order.

Zangl—and I am aware of once more making a remark critical of society—has been trained by upbringing and environment only to regard as real what he can grasp intellectually, that it, what our consciousness can grasp and hold on to, he thinks he only exists in his own consciousness. But because, in order to grasp supposed reality, he goes into the realm of ideas, he loses contact with reality more and more.

Only a confused person like him could suppose that his relationship to the woman he called "the one in green" had anything to do with love. He does not know, what we, with our ability to let contradictions lie and to ask no further questions, know very well, namely, that love is the readiness to penetrate the other, the stranger, and to recognise and accept that person the way he or she is, and to allow oneself to be penetrated likewise. But Zangl locks out the other, the stranger. He does not perceive, does not recognise, but projects himself on to the few people with whom he is prepared to come in apparent contact. What sort of person the one in green was we shall never know, because the only account of her that we have was written by Zangl. The objective reality in which he lived only gleams through very faintly, like a shadow, in his notes. Consider: a murder had to take place so that Zangl could feel a trace of reality penetrate into his consciousness. But it is precisely for reality that he longs, he is famished for it, it is what he is searching for in his erotic fantasies, admittedly in quite the wrong direction, because proceeding from a false premise.

From this basic flaw in his personality, this over-estimation of the intellect and this negation of what is chaotic and alive, stems Zangl's continuing hunger for reality; he will kill again, since the first murder gave him a brief release. Only dimly, so that he is hardly conscious of it, Zangl will at the same time have the feeling that his life is being lived for him without any participation from him. We shall see from subsequent entries in the so-called Black Book to what insane ideas on Dr. Kralicek's role this was to lead.

But at this point we are faced with the question: could the doctor have recognised this personality structure in his patient? Can we blame him for orientating himself round those realities which his faculties and his understanding revealed to him during his meetings with the patient? One can compare the situation in which Zangl found himself to that of a child who plays hide-and-seek and waits to be found, and thereby rescued, in a state of pleasurable horror. Zangl's tragedy lay in the fact that nobody missed him, nobody wanted to look for him, he sat—if I may be allowed the comparison—in the refrigerator and waited to be found, whilst the oxygen steadily diminished and the surrounding world went on unconcerned.

This situation, a person hungry for love but loved by nobody, is reflected in the entries that follow, in the description of his dream, in which he begins by noting down his relationship to language—words which reveal his intuitive understanding of the fact that a balanced feeling for life cannot be based on consciousness alone:

"That is what is special about me, that I have a faint awareness of what cannot be put into words. The word 'Whole' occurs to me. Maybe I should explain to Laurin that I had an intuition of the Whole? He'd think me downright mad.

I am a prisoner of language, although I make use of it in order to be free. At least I have my contact with Laurin to thank for this senseless effort.

On the expressive power of language, which I use, I, for example, at this very moment experience the following: just now a guttural man's voice speaks out of the air shaft. It says reproachfully: 'Insect powder! Obtainable at any chemist!' The speaker is the policeman who lives in the flat beneath me, a very down-to-earth person, but his reproach shows me how much he too is imprisoned in language. He uses the formula which thousands of billboards, advertisements and television commercials blare out: 'Obtainable at any chemist.'

Is he imprisoned? Perhaps he is quite different! Perhaps he doesn't even exist. Perhaps he is just put together out of flowery words and phrases, which a busy army of engineers have prefabricated and put on the market by the million in do-it-yourself packs. One buys the pack and puts him together according to taste. Perhaps nobody really exists. The assumption that one was a complete, unalterable human being once and for all would then be a gruesome mistake. And somewhere or other sits the engineer, quietly laughing to himself!

Imprisoned: in my dream last night I thought I was working my way laboriously into a concrete box. The walls are many metres thick. Air comes in through a narrow, winding passage with polished bends. The passage is no thicker than the width of an arm—too narrow to crawl out again. It is like an auditory canal. Oh yes, now I get it. I am sitting trapped in my own head, like last night, when I walked up to the one in green and calmly ordered 'Fire'. I recognise my head by the fact that the passage is an auditory canal. I gaze at the mussel-shaped end with longing, full of panic, and impeded from any attempt to crawl up it by the hopelessness of the situation.

But no: now that I am suddenly an engineer standing out-side, I see that this block in which I sit is made of ferro-concrete, blue and gleaming; and it is only the innermost kernel of a beehive-shaped temple standing under silently waving pines. It could be absolutely idyllic.

But this panic in the innermost part of the temple disturbs me very much. Because I am an engineer who has come in order to consider how one can release that shivering little heap of panic.

At best I could remove the outer honeycombs of the temple with pneumatic drills. Dust would then settle on the branches of the pine trees, and my ears would be deafened by the noise. But then, in spite of everything, the plan would ultimately be foiled by the innermost kernel. There the chiselling edge of steel would slide off the blue concrete in a spray of sparks, and injure only me.

It would take months, and help is needed fast! I could, to be sure, postpone the rescue attempt and start by boring a small hole in order to establish contact. I might even pump beef soup with noodles into the small pipe! Or are my borers too short?

Should the bore hole fail to reach me, then I could use it to blow the whole thing open: I'll fill it with TNT and bang! But then the huge blocks with their sharp edges would squash me, sitting inside. Only a little blood serum would trickle through the concrete dust and rubble, whilst silence and heavy clouds of white dust spread out under the pines and settled on my patent leather shoes. No, the only way is to blow open the outer honeycombs of the structure, lift the concrete kernel on to a heavy lorry and take it to a factory, where there is enough heavy equipment available.

But here under the pines there is no crane, no heavy lorry, no road to the coast nor a harbour there, no ship in the harbour . . . So one would have to build roads, bring cranes and a heavy lorry to fetch the concrete kernel, get it on a ship and take it, after a journey across the ocean lasting several weeks, to the factory in which the equipment stands ready.

Oh, how I hate myself! I beat on the concrete in a blind rage and scream: 'Do something then! Do something!' But I do not hear myself.

I am the prisoner. I am the rescuer.

I must go out right away and buy myself some nail clippers. I just can't stand these ugly long claws any more. I'm sure they must sell nail clippers at the station! (I will be careful not to go past the breeding grounds of those foul fungi. It would only irritate me at the moment.)

Buying: buying is marvellous. I spent hours at the station. Wandered round the kiosks and bought a lot of brightly coloured objects: colourful cigarette packets, the nail clippers —I started clipping while I was still in the station and the parings bounced off in large chunks—red and black plastic brushes, coloured handkerchiefs, tomatoes and radishes too, and a blue carton of milk!

And on the way home I whistled to myself. I haven't had such a great Saturday for ages.

Sunday

A smell of roast meat and the sound of organ music flows out of the windows. There are people going for walks in the park, carrying their bodies around. The black crows squat motionless in the branches outside my window. How much rubbish will pile up on me today, again? It has become almost impossible to control it with a pencil. Too much reality.

Lay in the heat of the night, like syrup. Brown bananas in boiling honey. Sweet, sticky, hot. Outside the wind rustles, distant voices float in it. Followed them.

(Thought about a girl at school, Helga, and her white legs sticking out of her gym shorts. Hadn't thought about her for years. Such a long time ago. It seems improbable to me that I knew that child. I am sure it was someone else, and his memory got into my gallery of images by some mysterious accident. Now she floats past my window with her high, clear voice in the night wind.) All the people in the park have no notion of my world! I live at a much deeper level than them, know more about life. But what am I going to tell Laurin?

(I can't concentrate, I keep thinking about the people who stuff themselves so greedily on a Sunday. Their eyes follow the serving spoon from the dish to the plate, from plate to dish, dish to plate: just keep on shovelling meat and gravy. Meanwhile they breathe heavily and make an effort to keep up a slobbering conversation. But they have to swallow spittle, so they lose the thread. Now they can only wait, eyes popping out of their heads, for the signal to start. Organ music from the radio. The whole house is echoing with the sound of cutlery clattering on full plates. None of them want to think, just to gorge themselves!)

How does a person think? An interesting question. One could discuss that thoroughly with Laurin. (I only have to scratch and a profound thought comes up. I'm a bee, getting honey out of muck!)

I wanted to deal with the subject the other day, because

sometimes I don't have an idea in my head. As though I'd fused. My brain won't stand it all the time. That is the curse of genius. Having to think all the time.

I must pursue this rather modestly. I don't want him to think that I consider myself a genius. And maybe I really am not one. One thinks in readymade moulds. Who makes these moulds? Who stuffs them into one's head? Thinking is nothing but a mould factory. Every thought is a finished, prefabricated piece. One can use it again and again. Sometimes this way, sometimes another way, like the movable scenery in a theatre. There are different plays on the programme, but the scenery is always the same.

I am going for a walk now, and afterwards to the cinema.

It is already eleven, but I am not in the least tired. The cinema is marvellous. One sits in the dark and outgrows oneself. One grows into an exaggerated piece of life. But above all, there is a beginning and an end. I enjoyed watching it straight through twice, first at five and then at seven thirty. It's easy to get in on days like this. And then people don't understand how much more worthwhile the art of the cinema is than sitting boozing out in the open. A really worthwhile film about a pair of lovers who speak different languages, cannot understand each other. How wise, how true. People don't know, don't understand each other—and yet do! And so sad. I love sad films. When it gets to the end and the music wells up! What a pity that one doesn't outline the underlying motives so clearly in everyday life. Music can change so much. In the car park, for example. If there had been music there as well! I would have had a far more beautiful recollection of the destiny for which I had to be the instrument.

Strange: everything about the one in green is already like a miniature, painted in black and silver. It is very reassuring that undertakers wear the same colours.

After that I went to see a funny film. And I laughed twice. And ate nothing all day except popcorn. I'm not like the others, who stuff themselves full of meat and gravy. And potato dumplings. Also drank a beer at the station and read the paper.

I really feel sorry for the gutter press. All the muck they rake up! 'Girl murdered in Prater district.' What a laugh! A murder is precisely what it was *not*. But they'll never be able to grasp a thing like that. An appeal for help with the search. At least they have understood that there was something out of the ordinary, because nothing was missing. As though one would kill to satisfy a low urge to steal! They'll never find the killer that way. Just keep on searching, you idiots. I wonder if the policeman on the floor below mine is helping on the case? He'll never get me!

(I now have the Black Book here, it's no good in the shop any more. A lot of things get in my way there. Fetched it immediately after and went home, to write the whole thing down in one marathon session. From now on I shall always write at home. As for the shop, I really need only keep that open for a few hours. What do I care about the others? Unfortunately I do need a bit of money. That's the whole trouble. Otherwise nothing binds me to them.)

And then this diary is no more than a continuation of Laurin by other means. I must not be unfair to him. I have bothered my head far too little about him! Without Laurin, no Black Book.

Monday
He really launched into me today. I'm still all confused. Although I must admit I was stronger than Laurin after all. He began harmlessly enough. I had already talked—as planned, about thinking. Really profound opinions. But he was not all that impressed. He looked at me with his head

on one side and said nothing. I started feeling very uncomfortable. I talked, throwing out the bridge of my ideas into the silent space between us in a creative impulse. But then I began to feel unsure of myself. A hollow feeling in the pit of my stomach, as though I had been talking rubbish. What was I to do? It is always an ugly feeling, when one has given of one's best and has still not succeeded in convincing the other person. Then his voice suddenly came from far away. I felt he had been deceiving me all along. Had pretended to be sympathetic, just to draw me out. Really coldly calculating, just amused at my eagerness.

'You always bring prepared material, don't you?'

I began to stutter. And what was it supposed to mean? But he immediately followed up the attack—still very calm —and accused me of never talking spontaneously. It was all very original and interesting, what I told him. But it was not genuine. I always talked so eagerly—he said—as though I was doing a tightrope act in front of a crowd of people. As though I didn't want to be recognised. I carried a flood of words before me, in order to hide behind it.

I wanted to say something, but he went on:

'And you prepare the flood well in advance. You laboriously construct it at home, weave it skilfully together, so that not the tiniest hole remains. What is it that you really want to hide from me?'

I must admit that I went red in the face.

'There, you see!' said Laurin.

Didn't I also have the feeling that our discussions had lacked conviction? They seemed lifeless to him, at any rate. We were beating about the bush. I should tell him what bush it was we were beating about.

I was quite confused. Because he is right. This moment, when I was supposed to talk about something I had not prepared, revealed as much.

Then he really put me in a spot. I should make a chain

of words, he said, starting with the word four, and say whatever came into my head. I said: 'Four, five, sex . . .' I went
red again and was unable to go on. But of course it was just
a slip of the tongue.

'Well?' he said, and smiled. 'Go on then, sex . . .'

'Sex, red dead . . .'

I again came to a halt. Too silly. I would have to go and
think of the one in green at this particular moment. But of
course I must not say that. That's my little secret. And a
grown up person shouldn't always wear his heart on his sleeve.

'My dear chap,' said Laurin, 'you'll have to explain that
to me!' But I couldn't explain anything to him, and I
hesitated a long time. I knew exactly what he wanted, but
I simply couldn't. I tried hard to find something else, I could
have admitted a connection between sex and love, love to
red via rose, and when it withers, the rose is dead. So simple,
but I could not, because the one in green sat there in my
mind and would not go away.

Really blocked.

'There's some sort of a block there, isn't there?'

Laurin looked at me with a touch of mockery. But it is
not so embarrassing, after all. He is my friend/enemy, but
more my friend, so I say: 'Yes!'

'You see!'

He manœuvred me with great skill, I must admit. I am
forced to admire him. A truly superior person. He is totally
my equal!

He began to develop his ideas on thinking to me. At first
I did not notice what he was getting at, but then the penny
dropped. He said a person could think or do this or that.
Things were only wrong if he suddenly could *not* do this or
that. This would be neurotic. Also, if a person *had* to do something. What about my walks, he then asked rather too
casually. Was I still doing as much walking? I said rather
vaguely: 'Yes, I suppose.'

Well, and did I perhaps *have* to walk that much? Was something driving me to it? Couldn't I do something else for a change, apart from walking?

But now I'd had enough. I blew my top, so to speak. I really went for him.

'If, doctor, you are trying to say that it is just as bad to do something because you are forced to do it through an inner drive, as it is not to do something because an inner drive *forbids* you to do it, then you are saying that the inner drive is sick.'

'Compulsive neurotic, yes.'

'So in your view every person of lofty moral principles must be a compulsive neurotic! What are morals but an inner law? The more aware a person is of the voice of conscience, the more it forces him to obey. No, you're pulling my leg. You think morality is a neurosis. And the only people you regard as healthy are those characterless rascals who turn with every wind that blows. Who murder in the SS and are now taking collection in church—just according to what the state happens to want them to do.'

He gave me that enigmatic look again. His calmness suddenly took the wind out of my sails. But he had no answer to that. He just commented: 'Why does that in particular get you worked up? I'd like to know why!'

Then it was four, and I had to go.

It almost seemed to me that it was his intention to cut me down to size. He went along with me the whole time, and behaved as though he admired me, and then he suddenly poured cold water over me. But he won't get me down. If he thought that this will stop me coming again he's made a mistake. I'm not afraid of him! Now I'll go there on purpose.

(And then I don't want to miss this hour every day. I need it for the Black Book. It stimulates me a good deal—in spite of everything.)

At this moment a terrible suspicion pervades me: perhaps

he has already reckoned on my reaction, that I would only start going to him in real earnest now? Perhaps he really is more my enemy than my friend. That disturbs me very much! And where does he get his knowledge of my most secret thoughts?

The whole afternoon, while I was clearing up in the shop, I argued with him in my mind. But tomorrow I'll go to him, if only to find out what he really wants!

And then: if he were right, that morality is nothing but neurosis, then it would contradict the theory that I'm a neurotic! Because I have no morals! It therefore follows that I have no neurosis! (My thinking is always superior to his!) Tomorrow I'll just go without any idea in mind. If he doesn't like prepared material—all right, then, I'm sure I'll manage anyhow!

Tuesday

And yet we worked extremely well together. It's very reassuring.

I did him an injustice. He does not want to cut me down to size and wipe his boots on me. What he says is not intended to humiliate me. He is also a fallible human being, although, of course, on a much higher level. He errs on a totally different plane. That is clear. He errs like a man of wisdom.

He asked me about my childhood, whether I was loved, whether I was lonely.

'You see, doctor, yesterday you criticised prepared material, and today you ask me about things that I don't know without thinking about them first.'

'Why not? I'm only asking you about what you remember!'

'I remember nothing.'

'Nothing?'

'No. I didn't exist before I left Constanze.'

'How come?'

'I only exist now. For me my past is like my future: I have to create it first. I think about it and it comes into my head as though I had invented it.'

'Well, then, invent!'

A curious experience: words are the rope ladder by which I let myself down into the cellar of the past. For example, via brass. On Laurin's desk is a sphere-shaped holder for his pens and his pipe. And there were brass balls on the terrace of grandmother's house. (I am very surprised to find this house and my granny in the cellar of my memory. Nobody can tell me how they got there: they are strange and at the same time familiar to me. But I say nothing about that to Laurin. Only report what I find, and not what I think about it.)

The smell of the hot brass, which reflects the midday sun, makes me almost dizzy. I smeared spittle on to it and watched it drying off. Spittle and brass steam up my nose, I couldn't have been much over three years old.

Brass also takes me into a kitchen with a large coal stove and to the knob of a handle which was used for opening the shutters in the mornings. Then the screams of monkeys come in, because the zoo is not far off.

Click-click-clack went the wheels of my skates on the warm red pattern of tiles in the courtyard. I went in a circle round bulging earthenware pots in which pink flowers bloom. You have to be quiet. Granny is asleep. Mummy is asleep when I bang the sword on my cousin's head. I wanted to kill him.

'We were playing soldiers. I took it too seriously.' But Laurin said nothing. So I go on. A spring has burst in my head. And the connections splash out: Ernest was the name of the Sawade boy, and I showed him the knife with which I promised to cut him up in the darkness of the mushroom cellar. He screamed with fright, and I found it fun to frighten him, but I was frightened too, but only of one thing: that I might suddenly change into the ghost that I was only playing at being. I was also frightened of Mrs. Panier's eye. But that's another story, which I have already written down: the hour of the birth of my God."

5

EVEN at the risk of exhausting the commission's patience I would like at this point to interrupt the flow of Zangl's associations in order to report that, contrary to all expectations, I have succeeded in checking and verifying his statement to the effect that he had already written down the story of the hour of the birth of his God. I found the manuscript at police headquarters, where it had been kept, together with the rest of Zangl's unsorted effects. Although the journals left behind had been looked through by the police authorities and the court, as well as the experts, from the most diverse angles, the manuscript does not seem to have been noticed until now as an important key to Zangl's personality. The police were of course primarily looking through his effects for material to explain the murder of police inspector Bernhard Leitner (retired), whom Zangl used to refer to briefly as "judge" in his diary, as a customer of the third case. Therefore we cannot be surprised that they left the manuscript lying unread amongst the technical diagrams of strange and mostly pornographic inventions. That it also escaped the notice of the experts can, on the other hand, only be due to their haste, because to an attentive reader this autobiographical story, undoubtedly genuine, provides a whole string of clues to his psychic make-up: if one only pays attention to the difference between the language of the journal and that of the story, Zangl reveals himself in the one as the defenceless shuttlecock of his own associations, who does not even possess his own language—in another part of the journal he himself notes this fact—but in the other he shows himself very much an individual who stands out from his surroundings, who puts a distance between himself and the object of his conscious act, masters this object and thus evokes the picture of a thoroughly normal person. But his description of God in his story, to mention only one further fact, shows us a child who, at a very tender age, is already pitifully lonely and without contacts, his development decisively disturbed by the early loss of the father figure, which later became an all-important factor in his sick need to identify with Dr. Kralicek, and almost led to the doctor's murder.

I hesitated a long time about taking up the discovered manuscript in my report to the commission, but I finally decided to do so for carefully considered reasons: I would like to submit for the commission's consideration any material which is in any way comprehensible, since the special interests of the individual members of the commission are as unknown to me as is the membership of the committee itself. And, moreover, it is not exactly clear to me what the commission wishes to clarify. Is it the question of Dr. Kralicek's culpability? Do you wish to know the sociological and psychological background of the case, in order to avoid similar events in the future? Or is it intended to base judicial reforms on this case? I do not know. Nor do I know why I was chosen to work on the case. My education in German and philosophy, my profession as a journalist, would seem to make me ill-suited to present arguments to lawyers or doctors, even if, as author of legal reports and series of medical articles, I am perhaps particularly familiar with the art of imaginative research.

Since the purpose of my work has only been vaguely explained to me, I take on the responsibility of making the report as thorough and comprehensive as possible. Whoever has commissioned me to do this work, I intend them to find as much reality gathered in it as I can lay my hands

on. For this reason I have decided to include Zangl's manuscript.

THE EYE

"Many strange events filled the days and nights of his fourth
summer. Once a goblin sat silently by his bed and blew white
clouds out of a clumsy pipe, until his mother came into the
room and woke him up. Another time, when he was playing
tractor on his tricycle—he was pulling tree trunks out of
the wood in the kitchen to the sawmill under the grand
piano—he suddenly saw, just as he was coming round the
wide bend of the dining-table down into the valley, his
mother, large and black, sitting by the window, carrying himself on her arm. This gave him such a fright that he rushed
screaming into the kitchen, to hide behind the broom cupboard door.

It was an oddly shaped flat in a gloomy town house with
creaking parquet floors and high ceilings. Through the net
curtains over the narrow windows the same dim light always
filtered, regardless of the weather, and allowed dark green
secrets to grow in the corners. The rubber plant in the living-
room sometimes wobbled sideways with its fatty leaves, as
though in a dream, and he was not allowed to touch it,
although it was so pleasant to run one's thumbnail along the
leaf surface and cut a ridge with a delicate crunching noise.

At breakfast on Sundays the room smelled of crisp rolls
and hot butter, and the little one greedily watched his mother
cut up her fried egg and put bits of it on to the buttered
roll . . . She used a spoon to pour egg yolk and melted butter
on to it, and if he could control his greed and keep as quiet
as a mouse she would call him over and pop a piece into his
mouth.

After breakfast mother would read out of the little holy
book. Each time she turned over the page she pointed to the

little drawings, and their delicate colours emphasised the mystery of the story instead of making it visible. Joseph and Mary on the flight into Egypt, and the apple tree on the branches of which hung the wicked Absalom. He had long yellow hair like a girl.

'Do you understand, little one?' mother asked in between times, and he nodded solemnly, because he knew that the book dealt with awesome things. And yet he did not understand how he was supposed to imagine God. There was a picture of him on the very first page, smiling out of a gap in the clouds with a beard and a kind expression, looking just like the old man in the house opposite who sometimes leaned, with his arms folded on a cushion, out of the window in the afternoon, but God had yellow pointed thorns growing out of the top of his head, like the chestnuts which dropped out of the high tree in the courtyard.

But God was something other than a mixture of the old man and a chestnut, because on another picture he was squatting in a burning bush, as though he was just doing his big business. At the same time the old grandfather stood in a mysterious relationship to the child in the cradle, which was also God, just like his mother, who could be seen standing by the cradle, and the white dove with the green-stuff in its beak. On the last page of the little holy book God was nothing but a yellow, triangular eye, remotely reminiscent of a fried egg, which, like God the Father, was also surrounded by thorns.

All this confused him very much, so that when he asked his mother questions or asked her to tell him more about God, he drew out the word as though he was trying to convince himself of the miracle man's harmlessness, because he was secretly afraid of him, even though God sent angels to guard his bed—an incomprehensible preference, when one thought of poor Absalom, who had to hang by his silken hair.

When they were out walking he asked: 'Mummy, where is God now?'

'He's up in the sky,' said his mother.

'What's he doing up there?'

'He's looking down at us.'

'Why?'

'To see if we're being good.'

Such answers did not still the nagging questions on the nature of the heavenly being. But he lacked the words to go on asking more questions, and the uncertainty remained, it spread inside him, was intangible but no less of a torment on that account. Above all it was the incomprehensible fact that God could see everything, absolutely everything in the world, wherever it was, so as to watch over it and silently control it.

When the little boy lay in his bed at night, after he had said his prayers and the light was switched off, he often doubted strongly that God could see him now, in the dark. Then he pulled the blanket over his head and asked himself whether God could see him through the blanket too. He almost believed God could not see through the blanket, but if this was wrong then God would notice that he was trying to hoodwink him, and God would be cross with him. Which is why he soon came out from under the blanket again.

He prayed to God: 'Dear God, please tell me whether I have made you angry.' But God said nothing. Perhaps it was necessary to turn to him in some other fashion. So Xaver first said the official prayer, which God would have to hear for sure, using it as a rocket to which he could attach his personal little question to the Almighty. But even now no answer came out of the frightening darkness, which was perhaps empty, or maybe filled with God's presence. Sometime or other sleep came.

In the mornings Xaver played down in the courtyard,

which was divided into identical halves by a wiremesh fence. On the other side of the fence lay the weird, strange world of a lot of noisy children, for the neighbouring house had a children's nursery in the basement.

Xaver never felt really at ease, playing alone in the yard, for he could not imagine what all those children in the basement opposite could be doing. In his own yard a little green door with dusty panes next to the dustbins led to the basement of the house. And on the small door was a large oval tin plate, with a picture of a frog on it. This little door filled him with terror. Full of awe, he called the animal on the door the 'Erdalfrog', without knowing why, but it was clear to him that this was the enchanted frog king, behind whom Mrs. Panier lived like a wicked tortoise in the dark basement. Sometimes she shot out of her dark cave and shook her fist threateningly at the playing child. During the long, lonely mornings, when he was playing quietly behind the door of the flat, the little boy often heard the heavy breathing of Mrs. Panier as she panted up the staircase. Thick carpets muffled her footsteps. Then he fled to the bright safety of the kitchen. Perhaps Mrs. Panier wanted to turn him into a tin plate on her basement door as well. But he liked playing in the yard if there were other boys with him.

On a Sunday afternoon, while his mother was still asleep, he met a playmate in the yard. The other boy had a scooter, and the two of them scooted round in circles on the asphalt under the chestnut tree. They played steamer on the dustbins and were 'dustbin men', by emptying rubbish from the bins into a cardboard box. The scooter dragged this trailer along with a scraping noise. Later on they made an excursion to the neighbouring yard.

There the auntie who ran the nursery lived underground behind white swaying curtains. One could stand by the window and peer with a beating heart into the semi-darkness of her mysterious grotto, the curtains billowing out round one's head. For little Xaver the nursery auntie was a fear-inspiring apparition, because he had never seen her and yet he knew the power she had over the lives of so many children. He could not imagine what she looked like, and he admired his playmate, who stood beside him, leaning in a relaxed way on his scooter, and allowed him to look at the mysterious home of the powerful auntie with possessive pride.

'Look,' said Xaver. 'Thweeties,' because he lisped.

With a leisurely flap the blowing curtain had revealed a china bowl full of coloured confectionery standing under the window on a table. His friend gazed inside in a day-dreaming way.

'Would you like some?' he asked generously. 'I'll get you some!' He propped the scooter up against the wall, leaned with his stomach in at the window and fished down into the depths with his arm. As he reverted to an upright position, his face red, he said:

'I can't reach. You try. I'll hold you!' Xaver lay on his stomach, and his friend grasped him by the legs. Xaver was a weak child, prone to illnesses, so that even then, in the summer, he wore thick wool stockings on his skinny legs that reached right up to his leather pants and were held up by suspenders fastened to a bodice which he wore under his shirt. Grey flannel underpants were visible between the bottom of his trousers and the dirty brown top of his stockings. All this clobber allowed his friend a firm grip, as he gradually lowered Xaver head first into an aroma of waxed furniture.

As long as the little one saw those round pieces wrapped in coloured foil as a goal before his eyes he thought about nothing but getting his hands on them and taking as many as possible, but as his hot little hands—how small they were, a whole bowl full of chocolates and such tiny hands—closed round the sweets he suddenly felt the blood hammering in his temples, and horrified, he thought he would never work his way back, that he would slip right into the trap and fall a victim to the unknown power that lived there.

He began to cry, whilst his fists vainly flailed the air, trying to find a hold, or help.

'Keep still!' hissed his companion who, gasping with the strain, was pulling at his legs, and finally succeeded in getting him back up and out again.

Each of them got two runny, warm lumps of coloured foil, which they peeled and hastily stuffed into their mouths. But they did not notice the sweet taste, stared at each other in alarm with their cheeks blown out: the afternoon had changed, because something unalterable had happened, and they were only just beginning to grasp that it could have been something bad.

Without any need for further talk they turned to run away into the other yard. Hastily they dashed up the stairs and crept, without any good-bye, each into their own flat.

Xaver played quietly on his own amongst his picture books and building bricks, without thinking of the ever-present control of God's eye, from which nothing in the world remained concealed. In daylight the oppressive vision of the night became unreal so quickly, strange and distant. But the uncertainty as to whether he had done something bad still tussled, while he played quietly, with the question: had anything actually happened at all? Towards the evening it seemed to Xaver that he had not been down in the yard that day at all.

But the hare cowers and folds back its ear in vain: with the sharp attack of the buzzard's beak the voice of his mother penetrated the semi-darkness before supper and found Xaver in his corner. With head lowered and toes turned inwards he pushed himself into the electric brightness of the living-room, where justice held court under the rubber plant: a box on the ear and off to bed without any supper. 'Nothing goes unnoticed, if little children are bad,' his mother finished off, in a warning tone.

What was really awful about the punishment was not being hungry and the pain, but the awful loneliness into which he was being pushed. Already separated from play-mates by his act: the sight of him was too much of a reminder of what should not have happened. Separated from his mother by her anger and above all by the question, what was her mysterious relationship to the unearthly and all-knowing power which kept a hostile watch on Xaver.

So the little boy lay in the dark warmth of his bed full of fear, and for the first time he became aware what it meant to be constantly under control without being able to perceive the controlling force. That night he dreamt that he woke up on a bench and saw a witch coming towards him with the intention of pushing him into the oven. But he could not move, his body was stiff as a stone.

The next day everything seemed all right again. Although there were more tears at breakfast, because mother scolded: 'Fancy stealing off the nice auntie from the nursery, shame on you!'

But later on she actually took him shopping with her and said nothing when he went behind the counter at the dairy and embraced the legs of the saleswoman with the words: 'Nice milk lady . . .' As always, he got a sweet out of the big glass jar for his performance. The jar stood beside the till and was topped by a thick glass lid, its lower edge rough and granulated as though crusted with sugar. How he would have liked to lick at it!

Contented, he toddled home with his mother, his index finger hooked into the meshes of the bulging shopping bag. Feeling that the world was once more clear and visible, he had no sense of the evil that awaited him. In the yard his mother met another woman from the same house. The little one was not interested in mummy's gossip. Small and unconcerned he stood beside her, he felt safe and secure and let his eyes wander abstractedly. They encountered the green door, behind which Mrs. Panier lived, and studied the frog. They wandered over to the dustbins and through the mesh of the fence to the window of the nursery auntie, which was shut now. The dark memory of something that had happened a long time ago crossed his mind. His gaze swung back to the frog.

But then he saw the eye!

It hovered behind the grey pane of the green door above the frog and was fixed unwaveringly on him. It was a cold, indifferent eye with a sharp, penetrating gaze, which sank like a ray of ice into the heart of the child and extinguished all feeling of security. It cut the protective bond with his mother and lifted Xaver swiftly out of his little world and into an unending space in which there was nothing but this little, helpless and shivering I of the child and the merciless It of the eye, that saw everything. In this way it had watched the children yesterday, had let them do what they wanted, had given no sign, no warning, no direction. Indifferently, it had watched the sin coming and being committed, it had watched the escape and the hope that nothing had happened, it had seen the punishment right from the start, had brought it about unnoticed but just as sure for all that, and now it was again turned on the little boy, cold and indifferent. The little boy knew, whilst he disintegrated under the gaze of that eye: so this is God, who judges without pity."

Without wishing to venture a literary opinion, I consider this story by Xaver Zangl as confirmation of the remark I made earlier, that we are dealing with a gifted personality who simply failed to bring an ordered structure into his life.

But let us return to the diary, in order to see how his mind revolved ever faster and faster, like a motor out of control. We left the diary at the place where Zangl was just noting his associations with the word "brass".

"A rounded brass arrowhead brings me to the blind horse whose leg was gangrenous, chapped and open and full of maggots. And I kept thinking, full of fear and horror, that this stinking heap of filth was a piece of a living being. I would have liked to take a knife to cut everything clean and smooth. I always wanted everything round me to be clean and tidy. I gave the horse some sugar to eat, and I lay down in the meadow beside him and pretended that it loved me. Shortly after that it was shot, and out of the rifle sprang a cartridge case of brass, hot and smooth, like the cartridge cases Antek used to make rings for his girls. I watched secretly in the stable. Like the eye of God always watched, specially when I was asleep. It only occurred to me this morning that perhaps God is everywhere, which is why one does not see him. Then it would not matter whether one said there is no God—it would be saying the same thing as 'God lives'.

And I'm saying both!

This morning I suddenly felt as though God was everywhere, even in the paving stones. (I went to the carpenter's shop to get some chipboards. I wanted to nail up the third case. And that's what I did. So I felt good: clean and proper. So that I functioned very smoothly at Laurin's. Now there's nothing blocking me, since the third case was nailed away out of mind.)

I walked over paving stones—this is what I told Laurin, without saying why I was walking over paving stones—and considered how one could explain to other people that God was in the stones. Perhaps I should pull out one of the stones, stick it under someone's nose and say: 'You see, cars run over it, you spit on it and wipe your shoes on it, and yet God is in it too?'

Then I went over the bridge and saw the canal, the water flowing, and thought to myself, if I look at the flow like this, then this image of flowing will waken something in me, ring a bell somewhere, cause a reaction, so that I suddenly see God in the flow. And then I thought that this flowing water is full of shit and used condoms, full of rubbish and dead cats. And is God in here too, in spite of that?

But how could one explain that to people, if one cannot explain it to oneself? If one does not even know whether it isn't just a nervous illness that one can see the flow behind everything.

It must be almost an illness, because one only knows that one's stomach exists when it is sick and gives one a pain. Like other people with their stomachs, I have a lot of trouble with the flow, doctor. Because as I see the flow, I am not sure whether it really exists. Other people, who don't see it, find it easy to say they have certain knowledge of the flow's existence. Because they don't see it. Even the vicar, who crossed the bridge after me, saw nothing but the stinking canal. Or else he did not even see the canal, because he was staring straight ahead and thinking about God knows what, only not about God.

'What do you think of the idea that one only knows about God, when one is aware of his absence? Those who don't find him missing can't know anything about him. They don't even believe. The awareness of unbelief is nearer to God than belief, because it rubs right up against him, whilst the believer hangs around at a pious distance.' But Laurin said nothing to this. I was quite excited and watched him with glowing eyes, but he did not so much as blink, just said:

'Is that so?'

Suddenly I said very loudly: 'Danger, enemy listening

in!' And then we both had to laugh. I was on the carpet again. I really fell into my own trap. Falling into a trap means being betrayed. Was I betrayed as I fell into my own trap? I shall have to ask Laurin next time, because it was four o'clock and I had to go, after I'd talked a bit more about my childhood, something to do with my religious upbringing. Because I was brought up religiously. I suppose mother thought it was better to be on the safe side. Twice a week, while she was at the hotel, a skinny woman came and taught me to pray.

I spent many more hours in the shop, until the thread that started with brass and pulled out whole clusters of images attached to single words finally snapped. For example, the word 'tantrum' (I often had tantrums as a child) made me think of the time I wet my pants, and this led on to schoolmaster Leise's pants, knickerbockers, and the awful smell in the classroom during my first year at primary school, and this smell is associated with my daydreams of those days, as though they were swarming bees.

This amazement at the day-dreaming child, who is somehow somebody who lives in me—even today—is mingled with the question, what this knot of words, which I like to refer to as I, really is. What is I, who am I? Will Laurin ever see me?

I can only catch sight of myself if I write fast enough. But one cannot write as fast as the thread runs.

One can only pull a few fragments on to the shore, as, for example, the thought that having God is as crazy as its opposite, not having God. Both conditions are manifestations of conscious life. Only someone who lives unconsciously, vegetates like an animal, will not see this problem, will not ask himself the question. So man is a totally neurotic phenomenon: he has been created in order to be mad. We stick labels on things and are content, we think that once we have stuck the labels on, described things, we have finished. But the word 'neurotic' says nothing at all. The word 'God' says nothing. I have a bundle of labels in my hand, and think I am holding life.

Wednesday

It's one good thing, to have killed the dragon. It's a good thing that his lair is now nailed up. I am now master of the dragon and the dragon's teeth. I have got my shop in order, and I don't need to go for walks any more in the evening. The toadstool colony leaves me cold.

And I read the newspaper in a completely different way.

A lot of lofty ideas come to me from the paper. Not the filth that I used to see.

But I must give a little worthwhile consideration to this: why do I call it dirt, what used to be, when I read about amateur photographers, the peeping toms, the orgies at Lake Wörther? Why do I evaluate those thoughts as filth? Because just as there is no absolute good, there can be no absolute filth. Obscenity, too, is something that happens between the hotel sign and the beholder. The obscene lies in me, the beholder, I make something obscene, because I find it obscene. For example, an orchid can be dreadfully obscene, if you look at it in a particular way. The hungry monkey, on the other hand, sees it as something delicious to eat.

What an intoxicating thought, that without me the world does not exist, that the whole of so-called reality is nothing but a tiny reaction of my grey brain cells to a stimulus, and this stimulus only occurs because my brain cells are organised in one way and not another. No doubt hundreds of people never notice the hotel sign at all. For them it has never existed, while for me it was a symbol that could not be ignored. The whole world is nothing but a symbol.

In the paper I read something about a Japanese sect that goes and washes lavatories. The members of the sect want to escape from the tension that comes with the fight for prestige. While the whole world slaves away after power and splendid clothes, they escape by renunciation of all prestige. And do not notice how they construct a new prestige, which gets higher the more they lower themselves, the more they touch shit. In their scale of values the lowest is the highest, and their life is just as much a fight for prestige as the lives of those people whose world they wanted to escape.

So this sect constructs a negative caricature of the rest of the world and obeys it just like my shadow follows me. One certainly should not strive. Because the fault lies in the striving, not in the goal. Because it is after all of no importance whether I strive after the greatest possible glory or the greatest possible dirt.

I have also got very interested in politics lately. I read about the shadow of the bomb in the paper, and it makes me think: white man is master of the world. Why shouldn't East and West wage war against China together? Should the master allow himself to be subjugated without a fight, even though a single planeload of bombs could wipe out the whole pack of yellow vermin?

Well, yes, but what about humanity? One mustn't even think a thing like that! One must persuade, not kill! Yes, but—whom to persuade? Nobody allows themselves to be persuaded. The yellow race wants to gain power, and that's all they care about.

My scruples—if the Chinese had scruples I wouldn't need to have any.

So I sit in my clean, well-lit shop and think this and a lot of other worthwhile thoughts about the world. The only thing that disturbs me are the fresh, light brown chipboards over there on the wall. Because I know what is behind them, and I know that I'm not supposed to think about them, and I think about them in another way, by telling myself:

'Don't think about it!'

So I paint a sign 'Closed on account of illness' and hang it on the door. I lock up and go home. There nothing stops me from creating freely.

Thursday

A cloud of nothingness keeps coming between me and the person that I used to be. This nothingness is like thick soup. It separates me from myself. You could also call it Time, amongst other things. Five days of Time is enough for me not to be the person who met the one in green. As I anticipated. If I had not written it down right away this experience would have sunk without trace like the whole of my early life. Between the brass knobs at grandmother's house and me stretches a bubbling sea of glutinous Time. Its grey mass covers everything up. I no longer see anything.

I read up what has been happening in the Zirkusgasse. I can scarcely believe it.

I have cut the reports out of the paper and stuck them in a book bound in red leather. On the first page I wrote: 'My Fight'. The fight of a white man against the dragon. If I had a photograph of myself I would stick that in alongside. And yet this is not life: it's paper and printing ink. It is not Time. Only the footprints of Time. I cannot grasp either my life nor Time. If I work hard I can at best make a collection of insignificant moments. However hard I drive myself.

This morning I drove myself into Burgenland. Hired a car and drove off. Wanted to be active, in order to collect knowledge. Rain, mist, everything grey. The street deserted, the surface bad for long stretches, and beyond a bridge a yellow sign: 'Burgenland'.

Suddenly a lot of vines to left and right beside the road, straight lines on dark brown soil. Huge black crows perched on the poles. A field with the heads of the slaughtered stuck up. I drink a beer somewhere or other. The men squat close together, speak in low tones, I don't understand a word.

Gipsy music on the car radio. Melancholy and yet full of life force. The sorrow in this music storms on ahead, taking every hurdle, like a rising tide. Later a talk on Freud. I learnt quite a lot. I am quite at home—it now seems to me—in the company of Freud and Schnitzler. I ought to read these people some time.

I am back at three. Because I have to go to Laurin. So that was Burgenland: rain, melancholy, wine, Freud, gipsy music, but not a single castle.

'You are trying to analyse me,' I said reproachfully the moment I got inside the door. Laurin holds his sides with laughing.

'What else did you think?'

'That we're chatting.'

'You can call it what you like. It's the effect that's important.'

'Can you see any effect?'

'Can't you?'

'What do you mean by effect?'

'That you change in some way.'

'What's supposed to change?'

'You yourself.'

'In what way should I change?'

'Become better adapted.'

'To what?'

'To your world.'

'What is my world?'

'That's what you'll find out.'

'You're not going to talk me into anything!'

'I don't want to talk you into anything. You've got to find it out for yourself.'

'What?'

'How should I know?'

'I'm beginning to find you spooky.'

'Why?'

'Who are you?'

'That's something else you'll find out.'

Laurin is so scintillating. Sometimes he seems like a sage, sometimes like a charlatan. Anyway, his questions help me to spin out a thread.

'Do I want to adapt?'

'It would be a good thing for you. I've also got a feeling that it's necessary.'

'Do you also think that I'm immature?'

'Who else says so?'

'Constanze used to keep saying it.'

'And what do you think?'

'I don't care. If it is immature not to adapt, I'm glad to be immature. It's all the same to me. Does everybody have to adapt themselves? What about genius?'

'You're a genius?'

'I don't know. I sometimes think so.'

'What gives you the right?'

'The work I'm going to do.'

'What is this work?'

'Myself.'

'That's the work you are doing in analysis.'

'Is that the path of genius?'

'There are many paths. But you are not the only one.'

'Who else?'

'Me.'

'Should that bother me?'

'You are free to leave.'

'Right away? But I wanted to talk about . . .'

'If you wish to stay, I decide what we discuss.'

I stayed. I felt quite weak. I seem to have found my master. Sternly, he ordered me:

'We will now talk about what gives you pleasure.'

'Yes,' I said in a small voice.

D

All evasions were useless. We soon got to Uncle Tom's Cabin.

But it does not matter. It only proves that there is something concealed under reality, and my ability to detect it. I don't want anyone to tell me that Harriet Beecher Stowe wrote out of humanity, perhaps even to fight slavery. Because when I'm reading I can detect the pleasure it gives her when the lash slaps on the back of the crouching slave. And they poured hot sugar into the wounds. Then the slaves used to sing sad songs in the evenings. Faithful and obedient to their masters. You could do what you wanted with them: they still bowed their heads in submission and suffered in silence. They call the secret pleasure they get out of it masochism.

(I didn't say anything to Laurin about the green one's suggestion that we should play master and slave. After all, I didn't fall in with it.) If one considers the social consequences of Beecher Stowe's scribbling—and the motives! It's enough to make you shrink away from the world in horror. Laurin agrees.

But to the world only success counts. Never the motive. Only for me, because I am so very sensitive. Strange, to remember that all of a sudden. I'd never have managed it alone. Laurin did that. He almost creates me, with his questioning look.

Master and slave: I had grown up and out of the schoolmaster Lieske's reach, wore a grey felt hat and occasionally paid him a jolly little visit after school—an adult visiting the scenes of his childhood. And in the garden, in the afternoon, I used to like being tied up. Cowboys and Indians was just an excuse. Later on everything was submerged, like Vineta. But when I am with Laurin I can hear the underwater bell ringing. When I cooked and drank ivy, because it gives you a temperature. But it didn't give me a temperature after all, so that I had to go to school.

'You like shirking?'

Laurin always draws such strange conclusions. Because I didn't want to shirk that time. Only intended to read *Headless Niels* under the bedclothes, until mummy took it away. At school, on the other hand, they occupied your body more than your mind. We often played ball games. And the headmaster's nickname was The Horror. I liked the games with Ernest Sawade best.

Later I soon became a serious person, read Jeremias Gotthelf —it took years before I could pronounce Jeremias properly. The first impression is always the most profound, even when it is false. And I carried sacks of corn into Aunt Gotnothing's granary. Hence my crooked shoulder. So traces do remain behind, even if the footprints have long been blown away.

'Her name was Gotnothing?'

'No, that's what we called her. She used to go round mumbling "I've got nothing, I've got nothing" all the time. Then she died in the henhouse. Like an old hen amongst the other hens. And she used to move her head like a hen, and claw with her hands.'

'Is there a congenital taint in your family?'

Laurin keeps going up blind alleys! Auntie had been married, but the general had been dead for years. Died up in the tower, where he used to sit for days on end, crouching behind his telescope. He was healthy. (But was he healthy? I can imagine him playing at an Indian campaign! His field workers as wild gurkha troops, marking out their advance with sheaves of corn, as though they were the corpses of defeated enemies.)

The rot was always in the people they married. That was usual.

'You don't like your family?'

Laurin always takes longest to make the most obvious discoveries. Of course not. I prefer strangers. When I have got to know someone it's already over as far as I'm con-

cerned. Laurin laughs. That was human. As for his family!
He had a travelling aunt, always came to stay for four weeks
a year. And then went on. Nothing but tittle-tattle. I find
it quite difficult to stop Laurin. Why is he telling me all this.
Do I want his painful revelations? He is only making me lose
the thread. Is he trying to be human all of a sudden? It
doesn't suit him in the least. Laurin in the rose garden—
with a travelling aunt! He should be ashamed of himself! I
hurriedly go on talking, save him from revealing and destroying himself. How could I go on respecting him? He might
even go on to dredge up a wife and child. Then the magician
would really be in the soup. (The woman who kept the
village shop used to sell square bottles of vinegar with
yellow labels, and the villagers used to put drops of it in
their soup.)

Now it all starts churning around inside me, far too
cumbersome to get out: the soup of the other general, who
ran auntie's businesses and died soon after, because he did
not have a stomach any more. He also used to hang round
the stables when Antek was there with one of the girls. But
I had a better spot. The general never saw me!

What a marvellous youth that was!

One of Antek's girls read my palm and said I would have
an unhappy marriage. She smelled of potato starch, and I
pushed her into the clover, but nothing happened, because
I don't do things like that. Bucks started up in alarm when
the moon shone and the shreds of mist over the Ghost Pond
really looked like spirits. The teacher who used to play
'Vienna, Vienna' on auntie's piano on Sundays and went
into his room with the cook during the lunch break was a
real buck. You could look in from the meadow. I often sat
in the trees and played birds. It now seems to me almost as
though this teacher also wore knickerbockers. He left soon
after, but not before the cook had made a hunting outfit out
of his uniform. She was clever at a lot of things.

But I was cleverer.

Swapped petrol for alcohol off negroes who were passing through and petrol for butter off the farmers. My brown uniform came from a train that had been shot up, and I played at being a negro by crawling round in the dirt under the mower and tightening screws. In return auntie allowed me to eat the solid food served in the kitchen—not so fine as upstairs with her and the general, but more nourishing. And then I could annoy the teacher that way: just with a look. Later I had to go back to mummy in town. I was really sorry. Out there I had lived freely in a way I was never to do again. Even after auntie's death her property gave me freedom. Freedom in my library. (The business with the maggoty horse's leg was much earlier on, in another life, with another aunt. I am only stressing that for the sake of truth.) Since then I have loved nature. A life close to nature is, after all, the most beautiful. Even if I do prefer thinking nowadays. But when I reach forty I may suddenly get the urge to go back to nature.

When I am writing I am always overwhelmed by pictures. Must point out to Laurin that for a person like me self-discipline is the most important thing, so that I am not overcome by the wealth of my own mind. I am so full. Before I threw myself on the bed and allowed the pictures to come I thought of the hut at the edge of the wood and the weir baskets laid out in the morning mist, when the fish jump. With my eyes shut like this I am a painter. Only I can't paint. But I wouldn't be surprised if I suddenly started painting at forty! At the moment my hand is still too clumsy for anything. For writing, just as much as painting.

I've no idea now what I told Laurin about the time at Vineta. Anyway, he let the session go on for an extra five minutes: I must have talked well.

Friday

The fact that I talk well is of no importance to Laurin. He follows his own rules. I keep misunderstanding him. He let me talk yesterday in order to reprove me today:

'You're getting off the point!'

I should have talked about what gave me pleasure. But I got off the subject and talked about Aunt Gotnothing. And today he reproaches me for it.

He seized the opportunity when I reported on the need I had for self-discipline, immediately after my arrival. (I wanted to tell him of the programme I had thought up: get up at six in the morning, a run round the park, to the swimming pool, gasping and sweating, at least an hour's swim, then massage and sauna—the whole morning devoted to physical well-being. A modest meal at midday, just an egg and an apple, and work for the rest of the day. My head clean and clear, creative work to the point of exhaustion. But he would not let me talk. Now the shine has gone off the programme.)

Instead he said hastily: 'Of course, more discipline. You avoid all the necessities. Now the question is: why?'

But I could not tell him, shrugged my shoulders. Do I have to believe everything he says? Do everything he says? I'm not a slave, after all!

(Formerly I would no doubt have liked to have been. Because I once wrote: 'I'd like to tell him everything. Really *everything*!'

He sensed the resistance, became serious.

'You are underestimating the gravity of the situation,' he said.

'What situation?'

'Your own. You are in very great danger. I'm beginning to see just how deep your problem is. You must not forget that you are being driven by uncontrollable forces!'

'Driven to what?' My suspicion was aroused at once.

'Who can know? But if it overwhelms you, you must ring me up at once, you understand? Day or night. We don't want anything awful to happen.'

He gave me some pills. I was to take them regularly, to soothe my agitated nerves.

What a lot of nonsense, I couldn't be more calm!

I am writing all this only for the sake of completeness. I don't want anything to be left out, just in case something does happen. (I'm a sexual neurotic, Laurin went on to say, a sadist and a masochist, with great communication difficulties, but very forceful drives, full of repressed aggressions—he really chose the strongest words in his vocabulary. But this sort of thing does not bother me, he won't upset me with that sort of talk, because I know better than him what it leads to: to lofty thoughts and the joy of creation. I told him I was going away and would not be back for a couple of days. I gain time in that way. For writing and action.)

Friday evening. This afternoon I tried action. With the judge, my most faithful customer. Now I am going to bed, to sleep.

Saturday

The judge is a little man with a pointed nose and a penetrating look. The skin on his face is dry and taut, except under his cheeks, where he has cushions of fleshy tissue as though he had little balls of cotton wool in his mouth. Round his chin, on the other hand, he is all wrinkled. There are little red veins on his cheeks, but his chin is pale. There is silvery stubble on it. Which is why his upper lip is precise and narrow, while the lower lip is imprecise and soft like a woman's. That's where he dribbles saliva in cold weather. His fingers—you can see that—would like to warm them-

selves between little children's legs. Sometimes he sniffs at
them.

His voice growls. He never smiles.

I was going to sell the third case.

I met the judge outside the shop yesterday when I went to
check up that everything was all right. I tested the locked
door. The notice still hung there: 'Closed on account of illness.' When I turned to go I found him behind me, wearing
a hat and coat.

'So,' he said, 'you're ill?' It sounded sarcastic.

He looked me over with his beady eyes.

'Come in,' I said. 'You want something to read?'

He followed me. I suddenly knew that he should buy the
third case. Then I would be rid of it and could get on with
my own life. He didn't seem surprised at the chipboards. I
hastily tore them down with a jemmy, or whatever one calls
that iron thing. Splinters on the bookcase, broken boards. I
kicked them aside with my foot.

'Buy it!'

'How much?'

'Ten thousand.'

But he just laughed. Nowadays stuff like that was worth
nothing. That—and he tapped the back of *Wedding Night*
with his knuckles—is only scrap paper now. You can get
written stuff in any shop, there's new stuff every month:
it began with *Lady Chatterley*, but now there's also *The
Carpetbaggers*, *Fanny Hill* and *The Story of* O. Whole
anthologies of dirt. The only thing of any interest now was
pictures, and even those were lying around in the street.

'Is that so?' I asked.

Hadn't I heard about the girl who was murdered in the
Zirkusgasse? She had a volume of pictures in her handbag.
Where did she get it from, do you suppose? The beady eyes
wandered over the bookcase. Well, there was no end to
inflation. Why was I selling?

Suddenly I was sorry. Not that I was afraid—even if he did harbour suspicions in his dirty little mind—what could he do about it? He can't say anything.

But I gave it to him for nothing all the same. The whole case. I just didn't want any more to do with it. Let him take it and go to the devil.

On Monday I shall deliver: three hundred volumes to a cold, musty bachelor flat on the third floor.

What annoys me is the insinuation that I am his accomplice in knowing about the third case. When even the best publishing houses! And what annoys me is the hypocrisy: if I lend out something of that sort the coppers are after me right away, for trafficking. But if the bookseller at the station kiosk sells it, then everything is all right. There is chaos everywhere, that's the whole secret.

(My library is like the hotel sign: it becomes offensive because of the way it is looked at. It is just that everybody is agreed about the way they regard me, whereas when it comes to the hotel sign it is left to the individual to decide what he thinks about it. If, in the near future, it becomes possible to buy anything and everything, nothing will be offensive any more. I wonder what people with a lust for dirt will do then? Where will a person like the judge go then?)

Sunday evening

A buyer came for the rest early in the morning. He didn't want the shop itself. That's another two thousand down the drain in key money. I shall give the shop back to the owner of the house, without seeing a penny for it. But that's the way of the world. The buyer has a lending library of his own, he wrinkled his nose at my titles and said it was a load of old rubbish. He came from Silesia.

I gave him the lot for five thousand.

That will last me three months, if I am careful. But now I am free and can devote myself entirely to knowledge. It's worth it.

I spent the rest of Sunday lying on the sofa, thinking. Now it is midnight. Next week will start under a new star."

6

LOOKING at the way Zangl's development is mirrored in his diary, it is noticeable that his descriptions become firmer and more real as his own existence becomes less real. He had, as we saw, not only loosened his tie with Dr. Kralicek, moving away from him and deciding not to see him for a whole week, but he had also shut up shop and given up his last link with the world of work and confrontation.

The sight which Zangl's visible life offers to our astonished eyes from now on is that of a person sitting silently in his own flat, without any contacts.

A process which began long ago with his divorce, and went on with his self-isolation and self-mutilation, has continued and come near to total isolation and flight from the world. The power, which we began by calling "the Dark", has taken further possession of Zangl, the way creepers take possession of a healthy tree and slowly throttle it. The murder of the one in green, a desperate protest of the repressed personality against this stranglehold, still has an after-effect and leaves Zangl with the feeling of being free for a time, until he again becomes aware of the deadly embrace. He still thinks he is living amongst realities. This is what gives his descriptions the shine of realism we mentioned earlier.

But the reality is only apparent. Because the real forces which control his behaviour remain totally hidden from Zangl's consciousness. The enemy, the dark force inside him, slyly provides him with apparent reasons for his behaviour, in reality leading to quite different goals, which remain concealed from him.

If, for example, he now shuts up the shop, gives it up and throws it all to the wind, he is not doing it for the one sensible reason, as any "normal" person would have done, namely, to conceal his tracks from the police. He himself tells us in his diary that he put a slip with the address of his shop inside the book of photographs when he set off to see the one in green. He learns from the judge, when he must already have read it in the newspaper, that this book of photos has been found on the dead woman. So it must be perfectly obvious to him that the authorities handling the murder case will at some stage come to him, if only to help establish possible contacts. I do not necessarily want to go so far as to declare with absolute certainty that Zangl put the slip with his address into the book in order to leave a clue for the explanation of the murder he was about to commit, even if I am convinced that this was the case: because I believe, as I have already said, that he killed and would continue to kill in order to give smoke signals to a possible rescuer, so that he could be detected beneath the winding embrace of the dark. But here, in the case of his shutting the shop, we have his own clear statement to the effect that he could no longer grasp reality. He is already a murderer running away from the police, and yet he thinks he is only throwing off the ballast of everyday duty for the purpose of thinking "lofty" thoughts.

Another example of such doubly motivated behaviour only recognised at one level shows itself in Zangl's decision to detach himself to some extent from Laurin. The reason he gives himself for wishing not to see Dr. Kralicek for the moment is his need to write in peace. In actual fact the doctor's remarks about his drives warned him that he was close to being discovered.

In the parts of the diary that follow we shall see how Zangl's relationship to the outside world became ever more unreal, even though to him it seemed to become ever more real, under the force of the dark side, which actually ended up by teasing him with the notion that the doctor felt caught out by Zangl, instead of vice versa.

I would like to make one more point before we go on reading the diary: Zangl writes with noticeable frequency of his need for order and cleanliness. For example, he thinks of a garden as made up of pure white sand, which he would like to rake smoother and smoother. He would like to cut out the maggoty tissue from the horse's leg, so that it is clean and smooth, he nails up the third bookcase with clean boards. We can see by a comparison between Zangl's real life and his deification of everything clean and smooth, that his devotion to cleanliness does not stem from any positive feeling, but results from his flight reaction from the dark: he is not acting in a forward manner in order to reach a goal, but is running away from something as yet unknown to us, looking over his shoulder. This clouds his vision with regard to the noble motives of other people, and we cannot therefore reproach him for trying to besmirch the well-known humanitarian motives of a writer like Harriet Beecher Stowe by explaining it as hidden sadism.

I make this remark to warn the members of the commission against jumping to false conclusions, should they be tempted to try to classify Zangl, in however worthwhile a manner. But let us continue with the diary:

Monday evening

"I engaged a porter to deliver the books. At the station bar. The porters sit at a table in the corner and play cards. Useless existence. They wear striped jackets like butchers, and red caps. Some are so fragile that one can't help being surprised. I asked for one with a cart, but they didn't want to know. Lazy lot.

I suppose it could have been my tone. I walked over to

the table, and because nobody looked up I said, more sharply than I had intended: 'Hey, you there!' I don't like having to ask people. I dislike having to molest other people. I know how it is myself. And then: 'Hey, you there!' I'd have gone on playing cards myself.

I was at a loss. A young, blond, healthy looking chap appealed to me most. He seemed strong and friendly as well. But I could not catch his eye. He was sitting too far away. But I was in a hurry. I simply find it inconvenient to stand around and haggle.

So I tapped an old, thin fellow on the shoulder.

'Pardon me for disturbing you, your worship, but might I be permitted to ask you whether you have a cart?'

Surely that was friendly enough. I caught other customers glancing at each other: why was a civilian talking at such length with porters? Stands at their table, bothers about them and simply will not move away. I could feel this question, multiplied many times over, boring into my back like pencil points. In spite of my coat. I think I was already blushing.

I had some books that needed transporting, from here to there, half hour on foot through the town, was he interested and how much would it cost. Revealing all my plans to a stranger's ears—not very nice. But the old chap eventually got up, after losing the round. 'Books?' he asked, 'not luggage?' Why was I transporting books and not luggage, was I moving, in which case he couldn't help, and were the books packed? Why only to be delivered? Was I a book dealer? In that case I must have my own delivery van! Take away books from a lending library—how come, you take those home one at a time, and not all at once. Did I read such a lot? Oh, I see, it was I who lent the books out—but such a lot at one go? I have sold them. That's different. How many were there? Three hundred, a whole bookcase, Jesus Christ! At long last he detaches himself from the table, where the others have been listening with open mouths and

stupid minds. He wants to haggle over the price more discreetly. He wants to broadcast my secret to the whole world,
but keep his own to himself! No doubt he had a good laugh
at my expense, even if I did not get the joke behind his
questions.

But then, who can understand porters' humour?

He makes a great to-do about getting a pencil out of his
jacket pocket, notes down the address, asks me for it several
times as though he were deaf, finally repeats it at the top
of his voice (and mockingly, into the bargain) for the benefit
of the whole room, while he is noting it down. I glance round
in embarrassment, smile too, to show the others how well I
am taking it, I can take a joke in my stride, but I only
see blank faces amongst the posh guests of the station bar, if
they are not in fact staring down into their soup or beer.
Some of them are smirking behind their papers—that is, I
presume they are smirking, because all I can see are the
newspapers over their faces. I really loathe public exhibitions.

Although I put my arm round the old man's shoulder,
call him 'my good man'—he remains a distant stranger,
impersonal. He even declines an invitation to have a beer,
although I would have had one with him at the bar. And he
would not come with me right away. Said he would only
come to the shop in three hours' time.

While I am waiting for him it occurs to me that he could
see the titles of the books, and I hastily wrap them into
parcels. They made up ten packets. I was very annoyed with
him, while I was tying them up with string. He had forced
me into making an exhibition of myself in front of everybody. I had to reveal my plans and my address and also my
attempts to get more friendly with him, as one human being
to another, he had rebuffed those very clearly, for everyone
to see. Dirty layabout. And he came four and a half hours
later, not three, as we had arranged. I won't give him a penny
more than we arranged, I swore to myself.

I showed him how annoyed I was, by being extremely curt when he finally arrived with his cart, attached to a bicycle. 'Ape!' I thought, when I saw the old man getting off his saddle in front of my shop. The vehicle was quite crooked and pulled askew—one of those carts where you sit at the back and pedal, and the loading surface is at the front. I'd have offered him some groundnuts, but I'm sure he would not have understood such subtleties. Then, in spite of my contempt, I carried out eight of the ten packets for him. He took his time, so that I loaded almost the whole cart. It's just that I don't like standing about, which is why I helped. Because I'm not a slave driver, like some posh people, and I'm not afraid of engendering class hatred either. Only I don't like giving orders. But the big ape just let me get on with it, so that I carried out most of the stuff. And yet I've watched porters at the station, they bow and scrape to the customers, old dandies in camelhair coats with mountains of pigskin suitcases—I felt ashamed on account of those rich people, because of the way they humiliated the porters. But as for me: what thanks would the old chap give me for treating him as my equal?

Then I walked alongside, while he pedalled. He pedalled with all his might, bent forward, so that the cart, squeaking and groaning rhythmically, was set in motion by the ape's tread. The old chap sat completely askew, like the entire mechanism. The red cap on his head.

I purposely walked faster than he pedalled, so that none of the passers-by would think that I had anything to do with him. How could I let an old fellow like him work for me? I ought to get on the bike instead of him and tell him to sit down with the parcels. And I would have done that, if I had not known that I would have had to explain the plan to him at great length and at the top of my voice, several times over, in a way that would have attracted attention, until people stopped and watched. But if it had been possible to do it in an unnoticeable way—I really would have pedalled the old man through the town.

Somewhere or other he got lost. Once, when I cautiously looked round, he had simply vanished. So he forced me to stop and wait for him. How embarrassing, with so many people walking past! But he didn't come and didn't come. Hate swelled up in me. If I had built the butterfly trap I would have allowed him to get caught in it. (Once, just for a joke, I wanted to run an electric current through the metal frame of the third case. The normal voltage would not have been enough, but I've got this old radio, I'd have taken out the loudspeaker and used it to step up the voltage. I think I would have got it to five hundred volts, so that even rubber soles would not have helped. And then everybody who used the third case would have been a butterfly. Little blue flames and the smell of singed flesh from hands damp with sweat— another butterfly less. But I never built it, and now it's too late.)

No doubt the old man had taken another route. I ran after him, thought of all the possible short cuts, but could not find him anywhere. Then I walked along the route where I had lost him and found him sitting on a bench, smoking his pipe. As calm as you please. I walked up to him—no longer friendly, no more of that 'my good man' stuff. I said as sharply as I could manage: 'What do you think you are doing? I've been looking for you for the past half-hour!'

But he remained quite unmoved. I should have told him the address. But since he didn't know it—what was he supposed to have done, after I had disappeared down a one-way street? 'I suppose you would have paid the fine? I've been waiting for you all this time!'

No wonder I get stomach trouble! I have to swallow so much rage the whole time. I just said curtly: 'Come along then!' And as we walked on I thought bitterly of the way he had added 'all this time'. Why was this ape lying? But the squeaking of the cart continued faithfully behind me.

When we climbed up the stairs I did not carry a packet. Not this time! The ape could drag the stuff up himself.

The judge opened the door in his bathrobe. The hole where he lived smelt stuffy. I suddenly realised that I had no idea whether he was a proper judge. Perhaps he was only some sort of official, something to do with the borough council or welfare. Perhaps he wasn't even that, just drawing a pension. But then he must have been some sort of official in the past. Perhaps he was a teacher? Or maybe the head of a lawyer's office? Newspaper office? Head of a tram depot? Camp administrator? You never know with strangers.

'I've brought the books!'

He reluctantly let the ape come in, left me standing in the hall whilst the ape dumped the parcels with a heavy grunt and disappeared down the stairs once more on his crooked legs. The judge stood in the doorway and examined me with his hostile little eyes, then he shuffled away, while I waited. He came to the door twice more to look at me, before the ape had come up grunting, with two more packets. Emptiness and anger battled inside me. When the porter had gone again I simply walked into the judge's apartment. If he had said something I would have snapped back at him, but he just looked. 'The carrier costs two hundred schillings. If you would be so good.'

It suddenly occurred to me that it was a cheek of him to let me pay for the delivery as well.

'But you are happy to get rid of that filth.'

What a nerve! How can he call it filth, when he was always hanging round the shop in order to borrow it.

'It's valuable,' I said. 'You're getting it cheap enough as it is.'

A father with his three-year-old son walk past down the stairs, the little boy in a red knitted jacket, chattering excitedly, his father in sandals made of yellow imitation leather, carrying a shopping net with milk bottles in it. He stares inside with a hostile look, without uttering any form of greeting, the child chatters into a vacuum because 'dada' is peering in at us, full of curiosity. He put me off. I am sometimes in good form with partners, but an audience shatters me. Ears on the stairs, bulging eyes—that really finishes me.

'You forced them on to me. Did I ask you for them?'

'You should be grateful!'

'What for? Do you think I like having all this muck in the house?'

'You liked it up till now.'

'One—that's different. You can hide it and enjoy it in secret. But a whole supply—you should have come ten years ago. Since then I've learnt how to go about this sort of thing. Not a penny.'

I picked up a parcel, in order to go. The ape was just coming through the door, with two packets under his arm, one balanced on his shoulder. His face was quite grey, bathed in sweat. I couldn't do it to him, I thought, and threw the muck into a corner. I leave in anger. My back would show him what I thought of him. I could hear the pig laughing behind me. If I meet him again, then . . .

The old porter was absolutely finished when he had dragged up the tenth. I waited for him down in the street. I almost felt sorry for him. I asked him amicably: 'Perhaps you would have a beer with me now?' But he was grumpy, pretended not to understand me, demanded three hundred, that is, two hundred as we had arranged and thirty for climbing the stairs and seventy for the extra hour it had taken because I had carelessly gone down a one-way street. I gave him five hundred. But he didn't thank me more than absolutely necessary. Just a 'Ta', and he was off.

Not a smile, not a kind word. Didn't even bow. Strange, that superior people like me do not command any authority over inferiors. A show-off, a snob, some rich, coarse idiot with pigskin suitcases—he'll get his bows for pennies. But I, with my soft spot for the poor and the oppressed, and my generous payment—I don't get a thing. I even find it embarrassing to give tips. Charity is so humiliating. And I am afraid of being reproached by the people I humiliate by tipping. I give furtively, ten times as much, so as to apologise for the humiliation which I have caused by tipping. It would be simplest not to give anything. But then I would be regarded by inferiors as a stingy, worthless dog. I wouldn't like that. I can't bear anyone to think badly of me. That is why I have to give. The only way to be respected is to step on people, bellow, humiliate the humble even further and buy them off with small change. But that is not my nature, I am too sensitive.

One just has to learn to live with the necessity of giving tips. Just as I would like to be lean, although I am in fact fat and heavy. That is something else I have to learn to live with, like the bomb and everything else in the world. (But I haven't been sleepy for a long time. Just physically heavy, while my mind is active.)

The low, worthless outer world, so-called reality, is so terribly banal. Living through this day with the porter has cost me more effort than writing it down. I was active—but what knowledge have I gained? Tomorrow I'm going to Laurin again.

It is the middle of the night, but I have got up and gone over to the desk to note down the following: it has suddenly become clear to me that I think it bad to have low thoughts alongside lofty ones. I wouldn't show anyone the Black Book. Only extracts, with the most lofty thoughts. Because I would always be afraid that my lofty thoughts would not be taken seriously, if they come hand in hand with low ones. I would like to isolate them, the good from the bad, because I fear that once my acquaintance with the one in green becomes known my power to convince would be diminished.

And I also think the following: the fact that this is the case is the result of my dependence on the Christian outlook. Only Christianity has made an intellectual division between the Devil and God. Which is why no whoremonger here is allowed to meditate on lofty matters. But if I had lived in ancient Greece, I would have been allowed to. But my mother ruined me by letting the skinny woman come and teach me religion. And so I turn away from mummy, just as I cannot stand the Christian God: both have burdened me with sins in the same way. They both tore me apart, each in their own fashion, and I have to run about cut in half, a cripple who thinks he can gain his soul if he betrays his conscience.

I have a conscience—what a surprising discovery. Why otherwise did I get rid of the third case, so as not to betray myself?

Three hours later: I got dressed and went out into the street to find policemen. I found some near the Praterstern and passed them several times. I also stared them challengingly in the face. But they did not want anything to do with me. Now I'm going off to have a good sleep.

Having visions is so beautiful: in them lies the true reality, unhampered by banalities. A little bishop in a red mitre stretched his little golden arms towards me as I sank into the sea of voices. I just had to add that!

Tuesday

Last night's thought must be elaborated today. I made some tea and ate a cracker with cream cheese: we intellectuals like having no body. Or almost no body, just enough for a cracker with cream cheese to be adequate.

Daylight, brightness—and the thought is still firm. How happy that makes me.

Because I keep seeing more and more clearly how divided I am, even more clearly than I did last night. And I ask myself what this I really is, which contains so many strange values, values like morals of Christian origin, and words it has learnt from others, thoughts that others have thought. This I would like to purge itself of all foreign ingredients, give up its conscience in order to find itself—and only finds that in giving up its conscience the self has also vanished.

This I—it seems to me—is only an idea that I myself make for myself. But I cannot make this idea visible without attaching it to strangers. So the idea of my ego has no bad conscience. I killed the one in green without a bad conscience, I used the third case without a bad conscience. And yet I did have a bad conscience in relation to that ape, when I let him do the pedalling, and a bad conscience when I looked the fuzz in the eyes at night. (Because of the third case, too.)

So I consist of two people, who overlap and interpenetrate each other, yet without having anything to do with each other and without being divisible: one person is the idea of my ego, but the other is the flesh in which that ego becomes visible.

And it seems to me: the idea of my ego could have been papyrus steward under Ramses the Second or temple guard at Quezalcoatl. But the flesh in which the idea of my ego walks about today stems from the time in which I am living, is alien and has nothing to do with me—except for the fact that it is me.

Intoxicating thoughts. I'm looking forward to Laurin.

Laurin was still at table when I arrived. I was too early. So I could sit agitatedly in the waiting-room and play around with my thoughts, as though they were coloured marbles. As though I was a child, and not a philosopher. (I also played joyfully with these thoughts, happy at my inner riches.)

I started when he came to call me, because his white coat was unbuttoned and an ordinary grey suit was visible underneath. And a smell of roast meat clung to him and I could hear a rattle of crockery in the distance. And he said: 'I apologise for keeping you waiting, but I got back late from my visits, and then you were early too.'

Whilst I was trying hard to serve up my thoughts as though freshly thought up, round and gleaming, he showed me the disturbing private side of himself, signs of his own, separate life, like his suit and food and what he did before I got there. But he was already buttoning himself up, and the whiteness of his overall covered the disturbing elements from this alien sphere when I sat down opposite him. The magician can afford, I thought with emotion, to show a banal human touch occasionally. That makes him even wiser.

Then I presented him with several things. He laughed gently.

'You must learn, not to live *in* your subconscious, but *with* it,' he said simply, as though what was getting me so worked up had long been familiar to him.

At that moment I would have liked to have been a carpet beneath his feet, also grateful for the fact that he was shutting off his own existence to be a complete Laurin for my benefit. Because I had realised meanwhile that he was also split, that in the depths of the house lived everything that made Dr. K., a family maybe, or a housekeeper, slippers and income tax return, the desire for a new car and bad dreams. But he shut all this off, so as to be able to be a symbol for me in his white priest's robe. For nothing more than a 'thank you' and a hundred schillings. Tears came to my eyes, and I wanted to give much more, I swallowed and confessed: 'My dear doctor, sometimes I'm afraid I'm leading you by the nose. I don't tell you anything about myself, only about a stranger—to be more exact, about a lot of strangers who have thought everything in advance that is inside me. I am acting strangers' material to you—can you understand what I'm saying?'

Laurin smiled thoughtfully, with his head on one side, whilst he said slowly : 'This is interesting too, the way you try to fool me. But I notice it all right.'

'You are not cross with me?'

'No, of course not. Because you are not trying to deceive me when you lie to me—just yourself.'

When I said good-bye he gave me a book and said amicably : 'That might interest you.'

And the other day—yesterday?—he saw me in the street and waved to me.

'I never noticed you!'

'No doubt you were too busy!' This is how he shows his benevolent interest, without trying to force anything out of me. Such a nice man. I can't wait to see what he has given me to read."

7

IN XAVER ZANGL views and opinions on reality are formed according to rules that cannot be more exactly localised. The picture which he constructs of reality consists of ingredients that, as it were, were floating freely in his consciousness beforehand, without us outsiders having been able to recognise with any clarity according to what system this unstructured chaos of reality was arranged into a picture of reality by selecting the ingredients from his own consciousness. The reality that actually surrounded Zangl independently of him during this process only played a fleeting part in all this: his searching awareness only selects what it needs in order to arrive at a foregone conclusion.

We have already noticed this phenomenon several times in the descriptions found in his diary, and it did not need me to point them out; but it is much more noticeable in his relationship to Dr. Kralicek. With Dr. Kralicek handing a book over to his patient we have arrived at a decisive turning point in the relationship, and for this reason I do not wish to miss the opportunity of drawing the attention of the commission to this phenomenon, since we are, in this report, concerned with the question of how far Dr. Kralicek could recognise and assess what was going on inside Xaver Zangl.

Right from the start Xaver Zangl was anxious to create some sort of order in the chaos of drives, wishes, lusts, values and contradictions which filled his soul, by making Dr. Kralicek a fixed point. The doctor was suitable for this purpose, thanks to the concurrence of many particulars, starting with the natural interest he showed the patient, and stretching to the outer framework in which he lived: this framework fitted Zangl's personal mythology, because, as we recall, he dreamt of a wise man sitting in a temple who in turn was dreaming him, Zangl, in a state of meditation. Well, Dr. Kralicek's house, which could only be reached by going through several courtyards, which evoked unpleasant associations, but which actually stood in an idyllic, peaceful little rose garden could, to anyone who wanted to find the temple he had dreamed about, undoubtedly offer the opportunity to project the images of an unreal, private emotional world on this combination of real facts. Added to this, we have the fact that it is quite common for the public at large to regard the profession of doctor as one that brings the holder of a medical degree in mysterious and ennobling contact with the mystic sources of being.

During the period when Zangl started his fixation on the doctor, he unconsciously tried to enhance Dr. Kralicek's person, by considering it as supernatural as possible. Once, when the doctor made some remark about his private life, namely, by mentioning his "travelling aunt", Zangl became downright angry, because signs of the doctor's human existence were being forced into his consciousness and this did not fit with his conception of a supernatural being. He expressly shielded himself from bringing up the subject of a family.

But this supernatural being, as the fixation became successful, constituted a danger for that destructive part of Xaver Zangl's personality, which we have called "the dark": as a supernatural being the doctor possessed the power to reveal the dark, to make it visible, and thus harmless. So the dark in Zangl started to turn against the doctor. Zangl begins to notice little signs of Dr. Kralicek's very ordinary humanity: there is a smell of roast meat in his house, under the white overall a grey suit becomes visible. All of a sudden Kralicek begins to show features which are far too human to be those of an out and out magician. Zangl's attempt to rob the magician of his magic shows itself, amongst other things, in the fact that he no longer writes out his name, but only uses the letter "L" when referring to him.

It transpires, however, as we shall see, that the fixation of the doctor in his role as magician has advanced too far for the patient to reverse the process alone, without the active participation of the doctor. On the one hand the person inside Zangl who is thirsting for freedom, clings to the image of the doctor as magician, on the other side the destructive person in Zangl tries to render the magician impotent, to degrade him to the level of a powerless human being. This vicious circle between two conflicting tendencies is ultimately, since it cannot be resolved, brought to an end in an unusual fashion, as we shall see in due course.

But before we come to the further developments in Zangl's relationship to the doctor, the judge steps into the foreground once more in the next section of the diary: the sexual drive which Zangl thought "low" and which for the time being had been associated in his mind with the third bookcase had in the course of events now assumed the figure of the judge. Just as Zangl had given the doctor the role of magician and brought to Dr. Kralicek all the demands one might make of a magician, so he relegated the judge, who was totally unaware of it, to the role of sexual symbol. Since Zangl was engaged in a desperate struggle against his sexual drive, the judge had no option but to assume the function of Zangl's deadly enemy. We can see from the words of his diary how all this develops:

Wednesday
"Started reading it without much enthusiasm, just a piece of homework, but soon got caught up in it. I lay on the

couch, entranced, scarcely breathing. Life would be wonderful, without nagging doubt. I am very like Jung. Some of the
sentences race through my brain like torpedoes.

It is Wednesday, and it is raining. Wet, heavy branches,
swollen with rain, green outside the window. I love dreary
weather, deserted landscapes. But rain only in green areas.
The sun has to blaze down in the mountains.

Yesterday, on the way home, I blamed Laurin for simply
ignoring my remark about so much in myself being alien. I
accused him of lack of interest. I was surprised that I only
noticed it after I had taken my leave. Or perhaps he did it on
purpose? I tended to think it was an oversight. Laurin seemed
careless with regard to me: he let me wait, then seemed
wrapped up in his private affairs, lacked concentration, and
was undoubtedly thinking about other things during the conversation.

I resented it on the way home.

But now there's this book: is it a silent answer to my
remark, or was it just chance that he gave it to me?
Would he have given it to me even if I hadn't made the
remark?

Such clever planning. It's wonderful, the way he makes
himself agreeable in order to conceal the ice-cold planning
with which he steers me along. Whether he lets me sniff the
smell of roast, like he did yesterday, or whether he appears
before me all in sterile white, like a magician: it has all
been thought out! What organisation! First he disappoints
me so much that I think rude thoughts about him—and then
sticks the book in my pocket, so that I have to apologise,
after having read it. I intend to admit that to him when I
go to see him later on. To be on the safe side, because if he
planned it like that he would know I was being dishonest
if I didn't confess.

If the idea was not so absurd I might almost think a large
part of myself had been thought up by Carl Gustav Jung.

That a human being can be thought up by someone else occurred to me even before I started reading—when I was reading the newspaper. (I often put off starting work by busying myself with preparations—I sharpen pencils, make tea, lay out paper in readiness. Or read the paper.) Came across a report on the memoirs of the Emperor of China, how he became a Communist.

Strange parallel between Laurin and the re-education officer: the same planning, when the re-educator waits with cold eyes for the Emperor to admit that he attempted to keep the jewels hidden in the suitcase for his own benefit, when they have known about it for ages. But when the Emperor does confess, wants to hand over the stones, he is met with a cool refusal: the people do not want the stones until he gives them wholeheartedly.

How little the outer world 'really' is! It only conforms to our internal concept. The Emperor's was totally changed, so that eventually he condemned everything he had once valued. And valued what he had once condemned. At the finish he was happily folding cardboard boxes, gladly scrubbed the feeding bowls of his fellow prisoners. A new person! A different person! The body is the one thing common to both figures, yesterday's Emperor and today's coolie. And where is the person who bears the name Emperor of China now? Is it in the mental personality, which has been destroyed, or in the biological existence which has been preserved?

What do I think of re-education? Is it good or bad? Would it have been better to liquidate the biological existence of that figure, in order to leave the personality unaltered? That would have been murder! But because they wanted to spare his biological existence they had to change his personality. That was contempt for human dignity! The democrat and humanist says: they should have left the Emperor the way he was, an emperor.

But as an emperor he did not fit into the landscape. They

would have had to lock him up. Would it have been humane to keep someone walled up all his life out of respect for human dignity? To what extent does an emperor have to be a misfit in a landscape for his dignity to deserve no respect? Was it so bad to make the Emperor fit in?

A word about the Emperor himself: should one have expected him to resist being made to fit in? For what reason? Is the personality of a useless emperor more valuable than that of a happily adapted shoe-black.

To what, I ask myself fearfully, does Laurin want to adapt me? And what sort of person will I be? No, I do not want this. I have a right to stay myself. Damn it all! How confusing when you realise that the 'self' is not absolute, but a function of social values. There is nothing absolute about it.

If I only knew who I really am.

At the moment it seems to me that being human means, in the first instance, being able to think. And the result of my thinking depends on the concepts I was playing around with just now. I myself depend on my concepts. But I have absolutely no access to things. Only to ideas.

And yet ideas are only a pretence, behind them chaos really reigns. 'I' am a sum total of ideas that other people have had. So I am just a pretence too. And behind me chaos really reigns.

The chaos that reigns behind me: perhaps that is just in my own head too. The world, on the other hand, is cold and impersonal. It does not care. And everything that occupies me and sends me chasing round comes from a handful of cells in my brain. Now I think that even the sound of the rain in the leaves outside my windows is much too lively to be natural. Nature, 'reality', is alien, cold, stiff and eternal. All movement is a figment of human imagination. In reality there is no movement, not even time.

I ought to write a novel about God. That would really be a hit! (Idea: I created God in my thoughts, and God is

the thought sum of all thinkable thoughts.) And then I'm
all for the Socialists. Because they're for planning. Secondary
schools and that sort of thing. The Christian Democrats, on
the other hand, want to leave everything in the hands of
Providence, so as not to disrupt 'God's design'. To me they
are an example of godlessness. They deny the close relationship between my thoughts and God. They let everything go
on any old how. Especially people who don't want to
'experiment'. I really must ask Laurin why he gave me the
book. Perhaps he hasn't got a plan at all. Now I'm going to
HIM.

I am torn this way and that. For hours after I left Laurin
and bumped into the judge as I was leaving, I was appalled.
But now I have calmed down again. What an absurd idea!
Why should the judge and Laurin be conspiring together
against me? It's just a coincidence.

I started off by having a good discussion with Laurin,
mainly about the unknown. He always sets me straight
again. He is such a solid type. He had no plan in giving me
the book, so he says, it just occurred to him on the spur of
the moment. He always manages to explain himself in a
perfectly natural way, and then his mystery suddenly seems
quite ordinary. Suddenly all the terror disappears, as he
laughs and says: 'Oh, get away with you! It suddenly made
me think of Jung, when you said the separation between
God and the Devil was Christian—and that there was an
alternative.'

'Why Jung in particular?'

'Because I was reading him only the night before.'

'That's funny.'

'It had occurred to me more than once. For example, your
lack of relationship to people you know really well. Jung
also says that he is only interested in strangers, and that he

soon gets bored with anyone he gets to know. And then your dreams—the cellar dream. And then . . .'

I interrupted him. I'd thought about relationships with people, I could explain Jung on this point: 'Man,' I said, 'is always seeking only himself, he wants to find a mirror. Someone one really knows does not make a good mirror, because the other's face will penetrate the mirror image. Total strangers are not ideal either, because the frame is too different. It is typical that nobody can imagine a being from Mars as other than somehow human: he always has a body, legs, and some sort of weird head. He is never a liquid, or a gas, or like a jellyfish, say. Human beings are always excited by remoteness, but a man is most taken with semi-strangeness. People ought to remain semi-strangers out of sheer decency. Anything else kills a relationship . . .'

But Laurin did not want to go into it. He tapped his pencil impatiently. For a while I thought this impatience a sign of his bad conscience: he wanted to justify himself effectively and I didn't give him a chance.

I thought this on the way home, after I saw the judge. But while he was tapping I believed—and now I again believe it—that he was only tapping out of an understandable desire to have his say for once. Not me the whole time.

By the time I had finished he was quite reconciled. He added: 'That's obvious. I'm surprised you find it so astonishing. Large sections of every person are part of a collective being. A mother sees to that when she orders her three-year-old to bow and shake hands. In other cultures she would tell him to do something else. The process is continued at school, with the ABC and the multiplication tables. This is the way the French Revolution, the Enlightenment, Kant and Hegel penetrate children's heads—but not only that, things that came earlier, Christian mysticism and even fragments of antiquity. So every caretaker is ultimately the product of a long development, if he tries to express himself.'

'A caretaker trying to express himself?'

'You mustn't be so prejudiced, my dear fellow, caretakers are human too. Just like you. Your thoughts about God, for example—do you know who thought like you before you did, even using the same words on occasion?'

'You mean my thoughts weren't original?'

'Nobody's thinking is original. In your case it was Angelus Silesius who said: I am as large as God—He is as small as me —He could not without me—Nor I without him be.'

'Fantastic! He said that? Angelus Silesius and I said the same thing?'

'That's nothing to be proud of. After all, he got there first. If he had not said it, you might have been unable to think it today.'

'All the same...'

'All the same, it goes to show that you are not as original as you thought. Not about other things either. In fact, I think you're rather old-fashioned. Fifty years ago people thought the way you do. Have you read Spengler?'

'Spengler?'

'Don't act the innocent. You talk just like Spengler's wandering student!'

The first time I've heard that name. I can swear to it, that I haven't read Spengler. All the more striking that Laurin should take it for granted that I was the student of some chap called Spengler. I am quite confused, my head is full of questions: for example, could one think in some other way if one thinks as thoroughly as I do, and how does Laurin know all this.

All I manage to say is: 'Are there more parallels?'

Laurin laughs at this and says: 'If you tried to find them all there'd be nothing left of you. I think we'd better leave it. After all, human thought is nothing more than a monologue that has been going on for thousands of years. Everything has been said before at some time or other.'

E

'But my language at least, the connections I make with words . . .'

'Just listen to your language for once,' said Laurin.

'What's wrong with it?'

'You'll find out for yourself. You're intelligent enough . . .'

I would have had enough food for quiet, concentrated thought, if I had not run into the judge as I left.

Grown larger with food for thought, I walked through the courtyards, I was already looking forward to the book and my pencil, hardly noticed my surroundings, stared at the ground in front of my feet—paving stones, kerbs, gravel—when I bumped into a man at the outer gate. He was hurrying too, eyes down, coming in from the street.

To my inattentive eyes just a black, faceless patch. It was only when I was walking along the street that it struck me: surely that was the judge! I turned round, walked back a couple of paces, peered into the courtyard, saw the man hurrying along, from behind just a hat and the bottom of his coat flapping against his legs. Met his gaze as he looked over his shoulder, the face hardly recognisable at that distance, but the gleam of those black beady eyes was unmistakable: the judge!

My first thought: embarrassing, that he should have seen me spying on him. So I turned abruptly back into the street, hid behind a panel of the door. I stood there for a few seconds—it seemed an eternity to me—until curiosity got the better of my embarrassment. I poked my head out, but the courtyards were empty. The judge was no longer to be seen.

Now I can laugh at the horror that came over me. But it is an uneasy laugh, because how can I tell which assumption is the right one?

I was immediately convinced of a gigantic plot: there was a secret connection between Laurin and the judge. They were hand in glove, Laurin controlled my higher thoughts, the judge my lower ones. And I, fool that I was, thought that the two ways of thinking were inimical to each other, were at war with each other, were mutually exclusive.

And all the time the two people who knew my thoughts were putting their heads together behind my back! Made fun of me! I upset myself, while they laugh!

But, I immediately thought to myself, who's to say that the judge and Laurin really do know each other? Perhaps it wasn't even the judge, just someone who happened to look like him? And even if it was the judge, surely he could have gone to see someone else in this gigantic construction of courtyards, staircases, landings, this gigantic spongelike structure made of stone, in whose dark cavities people have nested like strange insects, to produce smells, noises, and new human beings, unappetisingly alive? Who said the judge had hurried into the rose garden? And if he did, so what? Perhaps he's taking his dirty mind to Laurin for a cure? Another consumer of Laurin's wisdom, like me, although undoubtedly a far less worthy consumer. But surely it is unlikely that the judge found his way to Laurin by pure chance?

How does the judge happen to be in Laurin's vicinity, if there is no closer connection between them? But if there is one, then Laurin has known for ages about the third case, and I nailed it up and finally gave it away to no purpose! What I threw away has boomeranged in a mysterious fashion, and on to my clean side into the bargain—on to Laurin! It came to Laurin and revealed my secret purpose to him. How he must laugh when I keep burbling on in that lofty fashion —when he knows about my lower side.

My face burning with shame, rage in my heart, and dreadfully defenceless, I rushed home, incapable of thinking about anything else, at least to find a hiding place within my own four walls.

I fell into a leaden sleep on the couch. A complete change took place in me while I slept, my inarticulate excitement was replaced by icy calm, life came to my bed, snorting like a winged black horse: and when I woke up I knew that my urge to become myself—in spite of Laurin and the judge—was stronger than anything else.

I now regard such feelings as totally unreal, as pompous and immeasurably pathetic, since I have again spent hours at my desk. But I hold on to them and admit with the courage of someone confessing, that I had this feeling when I woke up.

Though I do feel inclined, now, to regard the whole thing as a figment of my imagination. One shouldn't go around seeing ghosts all over the place. There is a rational explanation for everything, if one thinks rationally.

The rubbing noise behind the wall, which is trying to annoy me, also has a rational explanation: my landlady is polishing her table. And not, what I think. What I am tempted to think, after I saw the judge and the nailed up room threatened to break open.

I sit at the desk and cling to rational thoughts.

Thursday

He calls it 'association practice'. We started off with it today. It's his new way of trying to penetrate me. I was too taciturn.

There's a rational explanation for everything. And yet there is a shade of reserve when I talk to L. now. It's expecting to maybe catch him out in some sort of betrayal after all. It could be a remark that shows more knowledge than he should have, if everything were normal. Or a strong curiosity which suggests more knowledge.

I sat on the chair in front of his writing desk, but inwardly I was on the watch. Not a single unnecessary word crossed my lips. Then he made me lie down. He adapted himself to me, and not me to him. I lay on the couch. I was to say whatever came into my head. I talked a lot of twaddle.

If he is hand in glove with the judge after all, one way or another, then this is a dangerous experiment. Because I am babbling straight into his hands.

I lie on my back like a dog and offer him my throat, and while I'm offering it I wait for the deadly bite. It certainly makes for tension. I can't see him, for in the first place I have closed my eyes, as he told me to, and he is also sitting behind me with a pad on his knees. I wait in vain for the scratching sound of pencil lead. In vain for the bite.

I couldn't even hear him breathing.

I burbled on about reading:

One reads this and that, and something always sticks. Often one thing contradicts another, but one doesn't notice that, which is very bothering afterwards. Because what one has read sinks down into one's sediment of ideas, and the contradictions take on a life of their own down there, confuse the unconscious, start their own warring factions, stop a person being in total harmony. The authors are to blame. They should agree between themselves only to write uniformly. Or maybe one reads the wrong way. You only read in a book what was in you before—pick out one idea here, another there. One uses books as a formula factory for foggy, unformulated thoughts which are already slumbering inside oneself. Has a person got time before he thinks, when this fog of thought is collecting? Then what we conceive of as our life, that is, thinking and conscious action, is not actually our life at all, but only a by-product. That means our life is controlled by the fog from the time before we thought. (I wonder whether that's in Spengler too?)

The question would be, who makes our fog, which later starts making us in turn? And then Goethe, too, said that one can only recognise what is already inside oneself.

So I burbled on in this fashion. I had to suppress other things, like the thought that I didn't kill the one in green in the car park, that I'd done it earlier on, when I couldn't make her laugh.

And I didn't say anything about the rubbing noise either.

'Are you satisfied with me?'

I put my shoes back on, after Laurin had interrupted me. I suddenly felt sorry that I hadn't burbled on about the tip: it would have been a simple reference which Laurin would only have taken up if he really did know something. I missed the opportunity to provoke him to a revealing reaction.

'You didn't really let go. All the same, I learned a lot. I think you read too much.'

'Too much?'

'You need a more active relationship with reality. Just reading all the time would make anybody ill.'

'But I don't read all that much. Not for a long time now.'

'What do you do all day in your shop?'

'My shop?' If Laurin inquires about my shop it means he does not know a thing! 'I've shut it up.'

'Shut it?'

'Sold it!'

'Yes, but . . . what do you do now? You haven't told me a thing about it.'

'Oh, this and that. Not worth talking about . . . I'm working at home now.'

'What at?'

'I'm writing.'

'A book?'

'You could call it that. A diary.'

'For heaven's sake! You mean you do nothing all day but write a diary? What in God's name do you write in it?'

'Myself. It's a continuation of our talks in another medium.'

'And you do absolutely nothing else now?'

'I can't even get that finished.'

'And what do you live on?'

'The money I got from the sale.'

'And afterwards?'

'Pardon?'

'When the money's finished?'

'I don't think about it. I've completely overcome my fear of the future. You don't have to worry about me on that score.'

'You want to sell the diary?'

'Maybe. I couldn't care less.'

'Do you think a thing like that would get published?'

'I don't think anything. Because I don't write for readers, just for myself. I note down life's hieroglyphics so as not to forget them. Later on I shall understand what they mean. Only a person who understands the meaning is a serious man. And for this it is necessary to have no profession, no money, no family. They just force one into insipid compromises.'

'Kierkegaard.'

'Pardon?'

Laurin explained who Kierkegaard was. He now seems to go all out to make me see how dependent I am on thinkers who have gone before.

Why does he do it? Does he want to degrade my ideas?

What's his special reason for bringing up Kierkegaard? Apparently he always refused to become head of a movement or to count as a reformer. He wanted to be 'serious', L. says, by just thinking. He only wanted to expose actual antitheses. No doubt something in Laurin's tone is supposed to arouse my doubts as to whether pure thought is serious— thought that wants to effect nothing, bears no fruit, that is, a purely intellectual game which has no consequences, because it rejects any reform as 'small-minded', as Kierkegaard did. For me—and to remind myself of it is very necessary at this juncture—pure action is lifeless, incapable of development. Mindless action does not give me a chance to comprehend my life. So I *have* to start by considering what I am going to do. Only considered action is meaningful, realises myself.

So I have to think.

But there is no end to thinking, to the consideration of actions! There's a counter-argument to every argument. You get deeper that way, it is true. But the depths are bottom-less. (Or do the depths only seem so deep because I have lost my sense of direction? Perhaps I keep going round in a circle?) The only real way out would be to make a decision and bring the thinking to an end at some point, by taking as gospel some conclusion I had just arrived at. Then I would have found a meaningless meaning, because choice is not meaning.

Can one live without the absolute?

Laurin concluded his lecture with the reference to Kierke-gaard. He asked if he could read the diary. 'The Notes of a Neurotic', as he said, laughing. I made vague promises.

Fell asleep at about six, slept badly, restlessly, woke up several times with a feeling that I was stifling. Then heard my heart beating slowly and heavily, like the fateful bell of Big Ben. Then sat rigid for a long time on the throne of rocks on the peaks of the Andes: awake, but not conscious.

Shall I give L. the Black Book?

Have just read what I have written. Wanted to try out whether one could hand it over to L. Strange discovery: one always writes falsehoods. It would have been better if I had written in the judge from the start. Now, when he is so important to me, I only have a couple of lines on him. Instead I made pages and pages of notes about the one in green, who is no longer important at all. Only invented stories possess a diabolical drumbeat which is also convincing. Reality, on the other hand, conceals the drumbeat under everyday things.

But this much is clear to me: one always puts too much emphasis on facts. For example, my lengthy description of the delivery: none of it is important. The only important incident in the whole undertaking is not mentioned, namely, that I met Laurin, without noticing him. No, facts are quite unimportant in life, it is only the personal evaluation that matters. I must avoid banalities and only write down my thoughts. If only it wasn't just the opposite of what L. suggests I do! (And yet I can't help thinking that all my brilliant utterances are nothing but camouflage for a horrifying nothingness! And when I read the Black Book now this nothingness—welling out of the book—collapses on top of me and cripples me. Reading this aimless stammering gives me a headache: I look out of my shell in the hope that this sea of formless thoughts, which is spreading inside me in such a merciless and deadly fashion, will take shape outside.)

A neurotic person—that means someone who is disorientated, a person with a lot of facets. Limited people have an easy time: if all you want is power you can become Napoleon. If all you've got in your head is sex you become Casanova. But the person who hides many conflicting tendencies in his heart—what becomes of him? Since he has nothing which could relieve him of choice, nothing but Laurin is left for him. How I curse prosperity! Because only the threat of extinction could force me to do one thing and one thing only. But this way—in peace and freedom—everything is possible. And so I can't make up my mind to do anything. If only I had to flee! I would get out into the world at long last! But this way I stay in my room and dither between this and that.

One's duty to the 'eternal values'—pardon me if I laugh! They are the means whereby the half-blind choose to allow the more useful amongst diverse tendencies to predominate. But someone with courage, on the other hand, abandons himself to them!

Which is why, for a disorientated person, there is nothing real about God, he is just the sum total of his own wish fulfilments. A vast abstraction that does not help him to make decisions. It is intangible, and cannot serve as a criterion. No doubt it reveals itself—but always only afterwards, at the end of time. Provided that there is still a consciousness which God can inhabit! For the disorientated person freedom is a burden, and so is the freedom of values, and the freedom of God. But who loaded him with this burden? There is no creator at hand whom he could make responsible for this state of affairs, where he is nothing, in contrast to the possibility of being everything. The only creators nowadays are authors: out of the grey, misty ocean of unending possibilities, of possible thoughts and actions they pick out a few and serve them up as firm reality. Although they limit multiplicity they win something with which they can deal freely. (Since they can take what sections they like and deal with them as they wish: would it be a good thing to demand uniformity from them in the sections they produce?) Am I an author, if I write a diary? Am I a creator? Unfortunately I am a useless creator, if I am one at all. For it is now not nearly enough to establish relativity, the way I am doing. It is much more important to say how one ought to live in it.

As long as I am unable to do this I must not give Laurin my book. Reading has taught me that much. And another thing—I use so many clichés, as Laurin has already pointed out. I write: 'As the light faded in my room'—a sentence out of the biography of an important man, Bismarck perhaps, or maybe Thomas Mann. At any rate a sentence which shows in cliché fashion how hard the person had written about labours. Into the small hours. (It could also be a book about

Frederick the Great.) The clean, well-lit coffee bar comes from Hemingway, in fact, so does everything which appears as 'clean and well-lit' in my journal. 'The ball goes to and fro' is distorted vernacular, and my image of paradise, namely, going through the anchor hole as a corpse is painted with the help of fuzzy hair from a Swahili moustache.

How much more alien material would I discover if I had an adequate memory and knowledge?

The question, as with the Emperor of China, remains: 'Who stuffed me according to some plan?' ''

At this point in the diary we find an entry which shows that Zangl felt, deep down in his overwhelmed normal self, what I have already mentioned in one of my comments to the commission, namely, that his picture of reality was made up of contents which had long been present in his consciousness, without his being able to order these contents in a causal chain which made sense to him—a causal chain which is only slowly and gradually becoming necessary, since he is heading towards a deed which he wants to justify as rationally motivated. We read:

"Outside the window black melancholy and night wind.

Suddenly, half-asleep, I knew what I had forgotten earlier. It slept indistinctly inside me, drove itself through my inner being, thrust itself forward for expression. The night is full of ghosts. How could I overlook that? How could I write that without detecting its meaning! Actuality no longer means anything to me, it seems. I mean, that Laurin mentioned in passing, that he had seen me in the street without my knowing it.

I noted this fact without thinking, without grasping its fearful significance! It means nothing more nor less than that Laurin knows everything! He saw me delivering! It simply cannot mean anything else, when he said: 'But you were so busy.' Only now, repeating these words suspiciously, I detect his devilish irony.

'Busy'—I take that to mean busy, because I was showing the porter the way to the judge's apartment!

Laurin saw me near the judge's flat. Too many coincidences, to be coincidences. No, there's method in this madness. The judge is in contact with L. No doubt about it.

What are they up to together?

I must get to the bottom of this.

I'm not going to allow myself to be led by the nose."

8

FOR SOME time now I have been aware of a certain weakness in my report, which I would now like to reveal to the commission. I feel bound to do so, having been honoured with this task, and I do not want to prejudice the work of the commission with reservations which I would consider it dishonest to keep from their knowledge. Up till now we have taken for granted the assumption that only Xaver Zangl forced strangers, without asking them and without their knowledge, to take over roles in the mystery play which had been written by an uncontrollable hand in the icy loneliness of his isolated soul.

But who is to say that a similar state of affairs did not apply to the other people with whom we have been concerned in our report, Doctor Kralicek, for example? Without exposing ourselves to this kind of doubt, we have up till now felt secure in the belief that Zangl alone was disturbed, sick, the mad producer, in a complicated fashion, of a drama leading to the death and destruction of others. But now we read highly credible assertions in the diary which lead us to guess that perhaps Dr. Kralicek also had a strong unconscious inner life, which caught hold of Zangl and forced him to take over a role which Zangl had no wish to play.

I am not bringing up this suspicion only on account of the contradiction between Kralicek's descriptions of his meetings with Zangl on the one hand, and Zangl's descriptions of his meetings with the doctor on the other. Because one man declares that they only had general discussions, whilst the other mentions the outer technical details of an obvious analysis, namely, the couch and a free association test. My assumption is not based on the suspicion that Kralicek is lying in his description, but the fact that the doctor gave his patient, at a specific and very decisive point in their relationship, a book which caused an explosive reaction in Zangl, namely, the first suspicion that he could have been thought up by someone else, as he had once dreamt, that a priest had dreamed him up whilst meditating. The very fact that Kralicek handed the book over quite by chance, without any deeper reason, when in fact he could not have given it at a more opportune moment, signifies, I am convinced, that in Kralicek there is also an overpowering and unconscious force at work, which conceals the real circumstances of his relationship with Zangl from him and leads him to actions, the consequences of which are catastrophic for Zangl.

I have to confess a suspicion to the commission which fills me with cold horror and a strong prejudice against the doctor: that is, the suspicion that something in Kralicek wanted to destroy Zangl.

At the same time I must point out to the commission that there are no opportunities available to me to investigate this dreadful suspicion, either to allay or prove it. Because, where Zangl is concerned, I have the diary to reveal his hidden impulses. Where Dr. Kralicek is concerned, on the other hand, we have no material proof, nothing which would give us an insight into his psyche without the censorship of his conscious mind. Kralicek is a man who is thoroughly integrated with the open, workaday world, who lacks both the time and vision to investigate the dark side of his soul with the care that Zangl devotes to this task.

If my suspicion, that Kralicek is also influenced by the dark side, should prove to be justified, I could not take the responsibility of ascribing blame in my report, which has so far been written on the assumption that Zangl was the only evil force at work. Because in this report we are penetrating deeper and deeper into the backgrounds of two murder cases, and we find guilt at each level, but in each case the condemnation falls on a different object, depending on the level.

With this thought—and I am expressing it quite openly to the commission—I am getting very close to the thinking of Zangl, whom we have all labelled as sick. Because he says at one point that all movement is a figment of the human imagination, while nature is eternally and rigidly the same. In this intuitively grasped situation, inaccurately formulated, we have I believe nothing more nor less than the point of view of the structuralists, that we can only perceive what the human brain is structured to perceive.

In my efforts to write a watertight report on the Zangl case I find myself confronted with the disturbing fact that many of Zangl's utterances seem to me to be very feasible, and that, to my mind, they can only be refuted by one argument beyond the range of logistics—by Zangl's actions. Because a murderer is never in the right.

In order to spare the commission any unnecessary consideration of contradictions in my report, I went to see Dr. Kralicek once more in order to acquaint him with the account in Zangl's diary.

The visit to the doctor's surgery took place on the 23rd September, about four weeks after Zangl's committal, on a Wednesday afternoon. The waiting-room was crowded with Dr. Kralicek's usual clientele: shabbily dressed, elderly women with careworn faces. I noticed one in particular, in spite of the heat she was wearing black knitted mittens, which left her fingers free. Judging from appearances they were mostly panel patients, with the exception of a little gentleman with a black beard, who rushed past me and out into the street as I came into the waiting room, so that I inadvertently knocked off his black Persian lamb hat. The doctor did not employ an assistant, he did the ordinary

administrative work on his own, kept the filing system himself and sterilised his instruments, such as syringes and
scalpels, in a little gas steriliser which bubbled away on the
window sill while he was examining his patients. No doubt
his earnings are low, so he may have been influenced by the
special fee that Zangl offered him, although he angrily rejected
the suggestion when I made a remark to that effect. The
surgery is not particularly well equipped, some of the
furnishings, such as the glass-fronted medicine chest and the
examination couch, seemed to have been old army equipment.

He gave me the impression of being nervous and overworked, smoked five cheap cigarettes in the course of our
half-hour conversation and when I asked him about his
family circumstances admitted, although I indicated that I
was not there in an official capacity and had no right to
interrogate him, that he was unmarried, but that he had been
living for the past twelve years with a woman who worked
as a laboratory assistant in the Vienna General Hospital.

"I had no idea about any of this," said Kralicek, when I
told him about Zangl's description of his visits to the surgery.
I told him word for word what Zangl had written down.

"This patient, Zangl, was a highly nervous person, whom
I tried to calm down to the best of my ability. It could well
be that I asked him to lie down on the couch. To make him
relax. And I might have encouraged him to say what was
in his mind quite freely, on one occasion. I would never have
involved him in a Freudian analysis. I simply don't have the
time."

The doctor gathered up the index cards spread out on his
desk and knocked them into a pile with a vigorous movement
prior to putting them back in his box, a movement that
revealed both uncertainty and the determination not to show
his uncertainty. "Time! We general practitioners have far
too little time. Did you see the people in the waiting-room?
The complaints of old age, malnutrition, complaints of

people who have been abandoned, who have no families or
any chance of social contacts. Their lives are sad anyway,
further burdened by illness. Accidents at work, genuine pains,
often sleeplessness, making the lonely nights endless. We,
the underpaid doctors, are supposed to have an answer for
all this. Then along comes a young man who is strong, able
to work, who ought to be supporting a family in order to give
his life some meaning, who in reality lacks nothing; and
then he goes on ranting a lot of philosophic rubbish which he
has picked up during his excessive leisure. I must tell you
that I felt no sympathy for the fool. I've just had another
one of those crazy people here, a person who has inherited
enough money from a rich father to avoid a sensible job. He
goes round with a beard, and dresses up like a rabbi with a
fur cap and an ulster. What's wrong with him? Nothing's
wrong with him, except that he's workshy and dreams that
he's lying in a wicker basket with a big-bosomed nurse coming through the door towards him, to pick him up in her
arms. It's absurd. She's supposed to carry him round the room,
a thirty-year-old adult! He wanted me to prescribe him an
opiate. He offered me money, pretended he had gallstones.
If I was really after money—but I've referred him to a psychiatrist. And I could kick myself for not doing the same
thing with that other idiot, that Zwickl or Zwangl, right at
the start. All these people waste one's time, and one goes
along with them far too much out of sheer kindness. You
wouldn't have got this sort of thing in the old days."

I am repeating the doctor's words from memory, but the
phrase "You wouldn't have got this sort of thing in the old
days" is still ringing in my ears. What could Kralicek have
meant by "the old days"? Even without a clear answer to
this question it is obvious that the doctor has a suppressed
feeling of aggression towards neurotics. I think it is mixed
with a certain envy of people who are not forced to keep
their nose to the grindstone.

He became matter-of-fact again when I asked him about non-professional interests. He seems to spend most of his free time reading specialist papers. A doctor, he said, never knows everything, new knowledge keeps cropping up which one had to make use of in helping the sick, so that one knows everything that can be known. One can only understand the whole picture of an illness in relation to the social conditions of the patient; even in dealing with accidents one had to understand the concept of being accident prone, the fact that certain people are liable to get themselves into accident situations given certain psychological conditions, such as anger, lack of concentration, and other superficial influences.

For depth psychology, on the other hand, Dr. Kralicek did not have much time. He does not believe in the significance of psychic processes that cannot be explained by everyday logic. "That's just a load of daydreams, escapism from the world of reality," he says. And he is by no means in agreement with the memoirs of C. G. Jung. The book was only brought to his notice through a review, he just "happened" to see it in a shop window as he was walking through town, he'd bought it, read it, had given the book to Zangl as the result of "a sudden inspiration" (the doctor's own words) only because he wanted to make the sick man see for himself that he was by no means a unique phenomenon, but a human being like any other, who should not think himself more important than any other member of the human collective. This is how Dr. Kralicek explained his action.

I did not miss the opportunity of asking him about the judge.

To begin with the judge's name meant nothing to Dr. Kralicek, but he found the card for Leitner, Bernhard. Yes, that's right, the man had been to see him a couple of times, but he couldn't say anything about the nature of his illness because of the professional oath of secrecy. But he could assure me that it had been a harmless, straightforward and commonplace complaint that happened to a lot of older people with a disturbed hormone balance at this time of year. Dr. Kralicek was very surprised that I should mention Leitner's name in connection with the Zangl case. He hadn't read anything about the judge's death in the paper. He wasn't in the habit of reading police reports, he said. He didn't have the time.

The catchword "time" reminded him of his patients sitting outside in the waiting-room. Assuring me that he would gladly make himself available to me at any time, he shook my hand and saw me out. At the outer door he asked me whether I thought that he still had to reckon with legal proceedings and going to court. The idea seemed to disturb him somewhat. I could not give him a definite answer on this point. I was grateful to him for not asking about the commission, on whose behalf I had visited him.

If I might give my personal impression here: Dr. Kralicek certainly did not resemble a magician. Looked at from a normal point of view, he was an overworked general practitioner in a district mainly occupied by the working class and old-age pensioners, by no means free of private worries, and who would have been glad to be bothered no further by the Zangl case.

This is my personal impression of Dr. Kralicek, gained at first hand when I paid him a visit.

But now let us go on reading how Zangl described the renewed grip of the dark side in his diary:

Thursday

"I haven't written a line in the Black Book for a whole week. Since I saw L. for the last time. What gives him this supernatural power over me?

This power always existed. I just did not recognise its influence because I was too blind to recognise its purpose. But now it has revealed itself because I rebelled too obstinately against that purpose. My resistance forced this power to expose itself: Laurin's aim is to keep me away from ultimate truth. But what could this ultimate truth be? I don't know what it is, which is why I don't know his reason for keeping it from me. How can I know the goal of a path which I am being prevented from treading by all possible means? Because during our last talk Laurin said that the most important thing for me to do now was to forget the diary and direct my gaze outwards. He wants me to lose sight of myself!

I refused. Not there, in his temple of roses, faced with his gleaming, be-spectacled gaze. There I remained mute. Sat with my hands folded, leaning forward, eyes down, and said nothing. But at home I wrote curtly:

'Dear Doctor, Circumstances beyond my control force me to stay away for the time being. Until then I remain, Yours, XYZ.' (He said I should work with my hands, for therapeutic reasons, as he put it. As though I needed any sort of therapy!)

Why does he object to my knowing myself? But at home the Black Book remained a locked door to me. I couldn't think of anything. Just sat at the desk and stared out. Or slept.

The sea of voices seems unending to me. It is too large for the perceptive powers of my mental eye. And Laurin has refused me his help, which I needed in order to master it.

And more. He secretly prevented my eye from seeing clearly!

I have been in a state of paralysis during the past weeks. It is as though Laurin had stuck a white speck in the middle of my eye. So that I am unable to see those things towards which I want to direct my eye. I only see outlines. If I want to talk about myself I look into a vacuum. Like a pit. And I fall into it.

For a while I tormented myself with the question—do

other people feel this way? But Laurin only put that idea into my head to confuse me.

I almost believe that the secret he wants to keep from me, is the truth THAT I DON'T EXIST AT ALL.

Such a horrifying truth, that I still hesitate to accept it completely. (How nice it was in the old days, when I still played jokingly with such ideas, like a child that has found munitions—without a notion of the horror that my toy concealed.)

Only the most extreme exertion enabled me to half pull myself out of the sea today on to the firm ground of formulated thoughts.

And yet this shore is only half firm: what I am writing down here is hardly satisfying. It does not wholly express the condition. Something unsaid remains and clouds the wine of knowledge.

And when I could describe the condition I am shy. I mean the rubbing.

The rubbing behind the wall disturbs me most of all.

This is what happens: I am thrashing about in the sea, try to create my environment in words, feel something slippery between my fingers, which are groping down in the dark, something which is firmer than the surrounding liquid —but before I can drag it up, in order to make it tangible in the form of a sentence, I hear the rubbing behind the wall again.

It is rhythmic. It nags at me, distracts me, the slippery substance slips out of my hands—I listen intently to the rubbing noise.

It's the same noise that one hears coming through every wall in cheap lodging houses, when people are copulating: a mixture of squeaking bedsprings, creaking wood, human groans.

In my case, though, it is not so lively, not quite so genuine. There is something artificial about it, as though it had been manufactured in a sound laboratory and played back on tape in order to confuse me. It is being played at me through the wall with a loudspeaker, to stop me formulating thoughts. And they know, through there, the effect that the noise is having on me.

In the old flat I was naïve enough to think that this noise coming through the wall at the most various times of the day was just chance.

At first I thought my landlady really was copulating on the other side of the wall. (An absurd idea, when you consider the age and appearance of the lady.)

Then I thought the noise was a by-product of her domestic activity: perhaps she was scrubbing the floor, polishing a piece of furniture, cutting bread, sitting in a rocking chair, or something of the sort.

So I moved out. That my room here was only half the price of the other one was an added advantage. (The fact that it is very dark bothers me less than the fact that the window looks on to the staircase: now I can hear human feet dragging up and down the stairs all day.) But the noise is here too! I heard it right after I moved in, after I had hung my suits in the wardrobe and shifted the table from the middle of the room to the wall, and also pulled the lamp across by the flex, so that I would have enough light to write. I had lain down on the bed, to prepare my thoughts for writing. But then came the noise.

I lay as though hypnotised, defencelessly exposed to the unexpected rubbing. It strode towards me like a princely lord who cannot be ordered about and who is surrounded by a court of obscene imaginings, drunk with power. The lord of this court acts as though he does not notice his courtiers' behaviour, as they spread themselves in my room with an inconceivable lack of consideration, jeering at me and making me dance to their pleasure, like evil-minded peasants making the village idiot dance at the village inn. At first I tried to protect myself by trying to imagine the natural sources of this noise, because it was clear to me from the start that it was only a symbol of copulation, and not convincing enough to deceive at that: it was too regular for that, and also—as I have said—too artificial. It could be a plane—perhaps a tenant was planing at his kitchen cabinet on the other side of the wall—or a creaking floorboard, on which someone who did sewing at home had placed a sewing machine. I also thought of a cat who had fallen down the chimney and was now scratching and rubbing in the narrow black tunnel in a vain attempt to get back up. But it was still rubbing after four days.

I didn't want to ask anyone in the house for an explanation. The people who live here, in these dark holes between unusually thick and damp walls, are poor, and bad-tempered as a result. I would only have exposed myself to the vermin by asking a question. They would have understood immediately why the rubbing irritated me so much, and they would not have forgiven me for my imagination.

I explored the whole wall with my ear pressed up against it, but could not discover the direction from which the rubbing was coming, nor could I make out more clearly that way what sort of noise it might be.

(And it wouldn't have made any difference; in a novel by Koestler the hero only has to press the nipples of his woman in order to have her in the palm of his hand. In the same way it is enough for me to produce an acoustic rhythm on the other side of the wall.)

It was only a short while back that I finally got on the right track. And it was this that at last gave me enough strength to pick up my pencil:

THE JUDGE IS AT WORK AGAIN!

In a flash the truth of the devilish plan became clear to me: because of the unusual acuteness of my intellect I got far too close to the kernel of Laurin's secret. At first Laurin tried to get me off the right track by exercising a direct influence on me, by forbidding me to write thoughts. When this did not work and I stopped seeing him too, he used his assistant to stop me exposing Laurin completely.

Although I do not know how far there is a connection between Laurin's secret and the exploration of myself, it is clear that there is a connection because of the judge's activity: he is always near me, so as to hold me down in the abyss of the third case through the rubbing noise. Through the constant appeal to my lowest instincts I am to be stopped from flights of intellectual thought. Technology has made fantastic advances these days. All you need is a little box, which the judge could easily hide under his coat, for the noise to be let loose on me anywhere. A battery the size of a matchbox even makes an electric circuit unnecessary. I could live in a log hut in Canada—and the tape recorder would still reach me with the aid of a loudspeaker.

I know only too well how these things work. Invented them myself, after all. The judge can fix his apparatus to the wall with ordinary suction pads.

Perhaps he came to see the lodger next door to me half an hour after I moved in, on the pretext of reading the gas meter, moved the wardrobe aside, because, he said, he was looking for a defect in the supply pipe, and fixed his little machine on the wall behind it. Now he can switch it on by remote control any time he wants to disturb me.

If I were not known to my neighbour as a neighbour I would now dress up as a gasman, without any hesitation, and remove the miniature apparatus. But as it is I cannot take this way out, I shall have to go to the gas board. It is all so embarrassing!

Friday

I keep having to remind myself that thinking is dangerous and requires an effort. It demands courage and is full of risks.

Because 'thinking' means defining oneself as an individual, to formulate oneself and thus forfeit some of one's common humanity with the mass of mankind. No doubt every person longs as I do to hide himself within a group. No doubt he also has a right to do so.

But, in thinking, a person is gambling with the possibility of belonging to a group, because his thinking could conjure up contradictions between the 'self' and the group, which force the thinker—if he wants to remain logical in his thinking—to say good-bye to his group. This happened to me a long time ago. I was made painfully aware of it at the gas board. It really is just the way the papers say: the individual doesn't count for anything in government offices. Nor does the story that the individual has to tell.

I knocked on the opaque glass pane. At long last the counter was opened, the official sitting behind it was still chewing at his sandwich.

'I want to make a complaint.'

'A complaint?'

'Yes, a complaint. A man pretending to be a gasman has installed some apparatus in my neighbour's room.'

'Gas theft? Please go to counter seven.'

'Not theft! Apparatus to cause a disturbance. But he pretended to be the gasman.'

'At your neighbour's.'

'Yes. A lodger.'

'Why doesn't he come himself?'

'He doesn't know anything about it.'

'About what?'

'That he wasn't really the gasman. That he installed some apparatus to cause a disturbance.'

'What on earth are you talking about, sir? What gasman, what apparatus? Couldn't you put it in writing?'

'I'd like to explain . . .'

'Explain it in writing. I'm busy. You can't take up the whole of my morning. Other people want their turn too.'

There were no other people. He had nothing to do apart from chewing at his sandwich with his cheeks bulging. Complaints about pretend gasmen could only be raised at the police station, if it had nothing to do with stealing gas.

(The conversation was longer, in fact, but I have forgotten the details. It was too infuriating. If one doesn't settle down uncomplainingly amongst the collective of gas consumers the gas board treat one as though one were subhuman. Anyone who doesn't fit into the scheme of things . . .)

It was the same thing at the police station. Only there the atmosphere was even more unfriendly: the uncomfortable guard-room with the grumpy official behind the desk, the others were playing cards in a room at the back, one of them was curious enough to come over and listen. As though he knew how irritating I found a third pair of ears!

At first they really were interested when I told them about the pretend gasman and the apparatus, but when I went into more detail (but I didn't explain too much: I didn't say anything about myself) they actually seemed to be laughing at me.

I'll just have to help myself. I'll tell the old man that there's a damp patch on our partition wall. The two of us ought to have a look behind the wardrobe.

The judge was cleverer than I thought: after I had chatted up the suspicious old man there was no wardrobe against the partition wall at all! Just a chair, on which lay some stinking clothes.

And I couldn't find a damp patch either. The old man knew nothing about a gasman calling, and nobody had been from the electricity board either. He just stared at me in a hostile fashion, grumpy and taciturn. When I put my ear up against his wall I could not hear any noise.

I have heard no more noise on my side the whole afternoon.

Was able to think undisturbed. Thought about something in the paper. If I weren't an outcast I would write the following open letter to the Bishop of Limburg:

'Your Reverence, You say that you are against state censorship, and yet you complain if the self-discipline of an artist is as minimal as that of this director. Whose art—you say—is atheistic and thus inhuman as well.

My dear Lord Bishop, perhaps you know nothing about that which we could call the torment of a human being whose world does not contain any God, not even a fellow human being. But there are human beings who live in such a world. Unfortunately, Bishop, you recognise this as one of the conditions which lead to the emergence of such "inhuman" works of art. What, in your opinion, could state censorship achieve? It could forbid works of that kind. That is true. But would the problem disappear with the prohibition? Has it brushed aside the assumption on which the work was based? Has it created God? Even you, my Lord Bishop, would not want to claim that. I know that you would say instead: It is precisely for such people, who suffer as a result of the world's emptiness and godlessness, that films of this kind should not be made, because they enforce their erroneous beliefs, instead of strengthening their faith and teaching them and guiding them back to the true path.

Without wishing to enter on a discussion as to whether the view that God is dead, is an erroneous belief—which cannot be discussed, if only because objective proof cannot be brought to bear on questions of belief—I would nevertheless like to ask you whether anyone has the right to prevent people from depicting their problems and their image of the universe. And if your answer to this question is yes, I would like to remind you that your answer must also be valid in your own case, for example, for your colleagues in the communist zone.

No doubt you will now say that you—and your colleagues over there in the atheist state system—are in possession of a special truth, from which you deduce the right to present your own picture of the universe unhindered, whilst you, on the other hand, are able to hinder other people by force from the formulation of their picture of the universe. That the view of the world as one that is godforsaken rests on an error which you have been chosen to correct.

All right: nobody will object to your trying to put right whatever you think necessary. Nobody will object to your thinking your own personal insight superior. But if you use force to implement what you consider your superior insight, you are involuntarily showing that your superior insight is in fact an inferior one. Because you show yourself content to attack symptoms instead of getting to the root of the evil.

Furthermore: expressions of a godforsaken feeling towards the world of the kind which this director produced are full of suffering at this state of affairs. Because what makes a man scream, if not pain? And he can scream silently too, without militant pathos, as you like to show.

So I ask you: as shepherd of a flock living in possession of the truth, surely it should fill you with satisfaction that those you consider to be lost sheep should suffer from the fact that they are lost? It surely comes to the surface in the fact that these sheep try hard to express their isolation, a lack which they themselves believe that you are called to eliminate.

If you meet someone who gives expression to his hunger, you won't make him any happier by forbidding him to express his hunger. It would be wiser to give him some bread.

Not censorship—faith is what the hungry soul needs. Even if I personally believe that faith is not possible, I beg of you, since you claim the opposite, to convince me of the rightness of your claim. I would be forever grateful to you and remain yours faithfully, XYZ.'

This letter made me feel much stronger. I shall try to get at the judge in another way : I shall watch him myself, in order to find out how he gets those noises through to me !

(Writing the letter out properly, sending it off and seeing it printed days later would be great: it would be a sort of proof that I exist. Just as 'My Fight' proves to me, when I am low, that I once existed. Because one's own existence only manifests itself in what one does in the outside world. But I won't send the letter off, all the same. Because my mind— if it exists at all—is not the sort that sets the world alight or enlightens a bishop. It is more like a little will-o'-the-wisp that increases the shadows round about instead of driving them away. As though I were a child wandering through a strange attic with a flickering candle: the beams begin to writhe, mysterious silhouettes creep closer out of the darkness.)

I am honest enough to admit that I don't want to attack the judge out of courageous defiance, but because, being weak and afraid, I have no other choice.

Tuesday

The outer world—if I once abandon myself to it—at once swallows me whole: I haven't written anything in the Black Book for days. Am getting on to the judge's tracks, drowning in his noises. It is torture when the wave of sound breaks over me. The judge is now defending himself with the noises. He can sense that I'm close on his heels.

(If the condition under which I wrote to His Reverence had lasted I would not have needed to pursue the judge any

more. It is strange, really, how much my life is a sequence
of conditions. My striving is still not quite lacking in pro-
gression. I change gear in leaps and bounds.)

I found out this much: the judge lives in a state of
regulated chaos. He goes to see Laurin every other day, at
four in the afternoon. I suppose that is when they are arrang-
ing their programme for me. But otherwise he comes and
goes at the most diverse times, in the afternoon he usually
goes to the public park, sits on a bench and lets the school-
children file past him. I have already watched him three
times from my spot behind the lilac bush. He mostly looks
at the boys. It gives me pleasure to see through him like that.

When I think of all the things I have already done in my
life: salesman, husband, librarian, pornographer, philosopher,
on public assistance (though I really have private means)
and now a private detective. In addition I am always an
inventor, neurotic, reader, author of a diary, killer of dragons
and a dreamer. Furthermore I was and am a seeker after God,
a creator of gods, an All and a Nothing, driver and driven,
prisoner and liberator—a bit of everything and not the
whole of anything. But then who is a whole, is the way I
look at it.

Admittedly the others affect me as though they were a
whole. For me the judge is the judge and nothing else. He
is a whole judge, so to speak. But what it looks like inside
him—well, I don't even want to know about it. I just want
him and his tape recorder to leave me in peace.

He lives alone. At eleven the concierge comes up to clean
for him. She leaves again at twelve, taking the pail of rubbish
down with her. There is usually not much in it. Twice I went
through the dustbins after she had been, poked about in the
judge's refuse but I couldn't find any clues. No tape wrap-
pings or anything of that sort. Just bits of leftover food, cold
potatoes, greaseproof paper, once some tattered socks as well.
Never any ashes. Apparently the judge does not smoke. But

perhaps she throws the stubs in the lavatory. Rarely does the judge get any post. Yesterday there was a newspaper that would not go through the slot lying outside his door. I overcame my inborn shyness and looked at it, although someone could of course have come along and caught me. It was a sunlovers' magazine, addressed to Leitner, Bernhard Leitner. No title or other form of address which could give one any information. Simply Bernhard Leitner. He always called himself doctor to me. A colourful personality. But he must not be too obtrusive, that's clear. On the days when he goes to Laurin he avoids the bar which he visits on other afternoons. The regulars there are young lads with oily hair. I haven't yet dared to go in, he might see me. I have seen one or two of the lads coming out of the judge's flat. Does he use them as messengers? This is the only possibility that comes to mind. Because so far I haven't seen him near my digs. And yet one or two of those oily-haired youngsters live near me. Unfortunately I haven't made a note of their faces. And I can't keep a watch on the customers of the bar at the same time as I am watching the judge. I took the precaution of staring challengingly at one or two of them when I met them in the street outside my house or outside the bar. They just laughed impudently in my face, and even turned round to grin at me afterwards. Meanwhile the effect of the noises is getting more and more powerful. Its effect on me is the same as smoking marijuana must be on addicts: right in the middle of spying I let everything go and hurry home in order to press my ear up against the wall, the floor, even the ceiling. Often there's nothing after all. Mostly I can just catch fragments of the rubbing, and only rarely do I get a longer sequence. Saturday afternoon is the best time, because that is when the floors get scrubbed or polished in many flats. Then the acoustic to and fro lasts a nice long time. At least long enough to send me off on my travels again.

I must admit I don't think as loftily any more as I did

that time when I wrote to the bishop. Thank God I wrote it down, or I would have lost it for good, and I would not even be able to believe myself any more, that I was capable of anything except listening in at the wall. I occasionally open the Black Book at that place. I can't read it, because it does not grip me and seems so terribly strange to me, so that it does not seem to have anything to do with me. But I am consoled by the consciousness that something out of my other existence is written down there.

How does the judge manage it? I boil with rage at not being able to catch up with him. Especially because I enjoy his nuisance so much. That makes me doubly defenceless. So the idea that he is exploiting my defencelessness fills me with rage more than the nuisance itself. The nuisance is quite pleasant now. Very, in fact. Why should that be?

Wednesday

Why pleasant, I have not discovered. But I have found out something else: I can't catch the judge out now because he isn't using his apparatus at all just now. There's a simple answer to a lot of riddles.

It seems to work this way: if I occupy myself a lot with the rubbing then I am dangerous neither to the judge nor to Laurin. The radio interruptions do not take place. After all, I creep along the walls of my own accord in order to enjoy the polishing noises as a substitute. But as soon as I withdraw into my hermitage to think, things become dangerous for them, and the transmissions start in earnest, with a particular objective.

So they torture me: if I want the rubbing I have to humiliate myself and crawl round the corners of my room on hands and knees, in order to hear it. But if I don't want it, they force it on me.

There is also something strange about the humiliation:

I don't have the least bit of a bad conscience when I crawl about and listen and imagine things. I put my whole heart into it, with no reservations. Only sometimes, when I imagine somebody might be watching me I suddenly feel very bad. Which clearly proves that the concepts of 'good' and 'evil' are not inside me at all, but somewhere outside. If I was alone in the world there would be no good and evil.

It is only when I remember the outside world, because I think that someone might be watching me, that my conscience bothers me. In my case my conscience seems to lie outside my body, as some abortive monsters have their hearts outside their bodies.

And someone torments me, by pricking the conscience that lies outside my body. But I can't see him. I can only guess that it is Laurin. Or the judge. Or both of them together.

One ought to do some research into the conscience business, but just now—so I thought—I could hear the noise on the ceiling. I'll lie on the wardrobe, that is more comfortable than standing on the table.

There was something, but I heard it too indistinctly. So I went to the chemist and bought myself a rubber force pump and a rubber hose. I took the handle off the pump and pushed the hose in the hole through which the handle had been stuck. Now it looks like a gigantic stethoscope, the kind that doctors use when they listen to someone's heart. I press the force pump to the spot I want to listen to, and stick the tube in my ear. It's as simple as that.

As far as the judge is concerned the state of affairs is as follows: he torments me all the time, either directly or in-directly. I must do something at long last.

For either I hear the noises he is transmitting; or I hear

other noises and wonder whether they are his noises or natural noises;

or I hear no noises at all and wait to hear noises at any moment.

In these circumstances the judge is always involved. I must think how I can help myself. I think the judge must be got out of the way."

9

CAN ONE consider Xaver Ykdrasil Zangl mad after reading his letter to the Bishop of Limburg? Are his notes on the nature of conscience so misguided? Surely what he says on the nature of the human mind applies to all of us, when he says that in its search for absolute values it gets no further than a little will-o'-the-wisp in a dark night?

Dark, overbearing pride on the one hand, the tormented feeling of his own inadequacy on the other, make Zangl the helpless victim of the forces storming in on his confused soul out of the deep, since he has stopped making use of the aids that we other human beings use. Clairvoyance and madness, correct insights and false conclusions drawn from them become more and more confused in a mirage of reality in which Zangl is no longer able to distinguish between the world which lives on without him and the shadow which he himself throws on the world.

More and more this shadow strives for dominance over things and drives Zangl to his next desperate deed. He notes:

"The thing about conscience: somehow I would like to have formulated the idea that conscience does not belong naturally to me at all. Someone has slyly attached it to me afterwards, because he liked tormenting me. Now, every time that I feel, think, or do something, I do not know whether it is really me who is feeling, thinking or doing it, or whether it was some alien body who was inserted later on. (I've got the feeling that I have already said something of the sort. But I no longer know what I have already written and what

I only thought.) And I no longer have any idea of time: mummy giving me a hiding seems more recent than the obscure business with the one in green, about whom I no longer remember anything precise for the time being. I am like a sandwich, that means, arranged in layers going horizontally through time. My momentary feeling of self is determined by the position of my consciousness within the layers. Sometimes it is in the smack-bottom-layer, sometimes in the layer of knowledge, sometimes in the animal layer (the place where I am merely biological, that means eating or sleeping). Now the animal layer mostly happens after I have been listening. But who decides where my consciousness is to be? Somebody must steer it from outside! It is not possible any other way. I must bring this helplessness to an end!

Thursday

I went to the judge. It suddenly came over me and I just went. Why didn't I think of it right away? The human soul is a riddle.

If the judge had not been at home—it might all have turned out differently. Then I would not be so calm now. But it is really better this way. Because I have freed myself from him.

'Stop your damned transmissions,' I said to him right at the door.

He had opened it hesitantly, was wearing slippers and a greasy dressing-gown, unshaved and dirty. But I pushed the door open and walked into his place, into the dragon's cave. This unexpected courage makes me proud and happy, happy and proud.

The judge pretended not to understand.

'What transmissions?'

'The filthy things you play off your tape recorder, in order to irritate me.'

'Are you mad?'

'That would suit you, wouldn't it? You and Laurin. Stop it, or . . .'

'Leave my flat or . . .'

'Or?'

'I'll send for the police!'

'You can't expect the police to give you any protection for that sort of thing.'

He changed his tune immediately, became quite small, backed away in terror. Something grew inside me. A marvellous feeling of superiority. He really was too small, too pitiful. And yet I would not have hit him, if he hadn't stumbled at the threshold to his room.

Because as I grew larger and larger, became stronger and slowly advanced towards him, he kept getting smaller and retreated. At the threshold—going backwards—he stumbled. Fell backwards. Knocked down an old flower stand behind the door.

His terror was pitiful! This creature, who thought he could dominate me—now he was lying on the ground at my feet. Blinked up at me with his beady eyes, usually so authoritative.

'What do you want of me, what's got into you, I really haven't done anything . . .'

Smack—I gave him one. I leaned over him and smacked my hand across his face. Blood ran out of his nose, but he did not move, stared at me, horrified.

It is great, spreading horror. People like us have far too little opportunity for it, I think now. I had never been allowed to arouse horror, I was always the one who was horrified. What power a person can have, without ever suspecting it.

'The tape recorder, the transmitter, the tapes,' I barked at him. (I was still holding back, although I would like to have provoked more horror, to the bitter end.)

But he just whimpered. It sounded like whimpering, but if you listened carefully it was abuse.

That really was going too far. If he had begged—I don't know what I would have done.

But as it was I knocked in his head with the flower stand. I was filled with revulsion as I saw the blood and all the mess, but the revulsion gave me the right impetus. It is marvellous, being able to really loathe someone from the bottom of your heart. Usually one is inhibited by all sorts of thoughts—you tell yourself: there is something in it, it is partly my fault. Or: he didn't know what he was doing. But when you abandon yourself totally to a situation, and a wave of loathing rises in one, and one lets it rise and rise, until one stands there like the archangel with the flaming sword, destroying and stamping out all vermin, all the filth in the world—a great feeling, heroic, in fact. Unfortunately my trousers were covered in blood, afterwards. (Should I really confide all this to my diary? So what, I am courageous, look at myself squarely, do not try to conceal myself.)

The flower stand was shaped like a huge, elongated hour-glass, tall and thin, with wooden semi-spheres at top and bottom, the flat surface of the top one for putting down the flower pot, the bottom one served as a foot. Suddenly, as I was bringing it down again and again with all my might, I could not help thinking of the workmen who pave roads. They also have pounders like that, which they use for banging cobblestones into sand.

That made me laugh. In spite of my weariness. I was really exhausted, but inside I felt clear and calm. (I avoid writing 'clean and well-lit' now. I want, yes, I *want* my own language.) All I wanted was a cigarette, a small Turkish coffee and the smile of a friendly waiter.

Well, the waiter did not smile, but the Turkish coffee was hot and strong. No doubt I needed it mainly because I did not want to think 'clean and well-lit'—that way, with the coffee, the café came into it anyhow. It just isn't that easy to shake off alien elements in ourselves.

In the café it occurred to me for the first time that I had completely forgotten to look for the tape recorder. I had not bothered to look round the judge's flat at all, not for anything else either. I was surprised at myself, that all this should suddenly be a matter of complete indifference to me. All the rubbing, and so on. When I got home I immediately threw away the rubber pump that I had bought for listening in. I cut up the hose into little pieces and washed them down the drain. Then I went to the cinema.

For the first time in ages I can look forward to a peaceful night. That is precious to me.

Friday

Again and again I learn from bitter experience that I am an above-average human being. I only have to drift along in the current of life for a few hours, and it is scarcely possible to work on what I have gained. I shall have to regulate my contacts with the outer world more carefully. Otherwise I drown too quickly in the chaos of facts. For example, this train journey to Linz, so much to note down and keep hold of, so that it does not sink down again and elude my grasp.

It began with a walk to the station, yesterday evening. Because it is at the station that they throw out the first newspapers for people to read. Still wet from the presses, so that one's fingers go black, if you leaf through them looking for your own tracks. Found my tracks on page three, a headline across two columns, between traffic problems and the opening of a nursery. Really given too little attention, when you consider the significance of the deed. But the significance does not reveal itself to hasty, ordinary people. The description was as distorted as it could be.

And yet it interested me. Reading between the lines, you could see that people were proud of their town's rising crime rate. Drew parallels with metropolises like London and Paris. Now they have their own murderer too. Somehow people are grateful to me, without of course being aware of it. And they ought to be grateful to me, but really they shouldn't thank me for putting their town's crime rate up, but for the destruction of evil. These poor Viennese are the victims of their own mistake, I feel sorry for them, like the rescued man who thanks me for having sent him flowers which I did not send at all, whilst he knows nothing of what he should really thank me for: his rescue.

This distorted situation must be put right. Had they only spat hatred against the assumed murderer—then I would simply have punished them with silent scorn. But now I put pen to paper.

At the main post office they have pens hanging on the ends of chains, and there, sitting at one of the desks, I wrote to the newspaper about the true state of affairs: that it wasn't a boy prostitute who killed his lover and then made a run for it, but that it had been a manly, necessary, and liberating act. It had nothing to do with homosexual circles, as was mistakenly supposed, but was the victory of light over the dragon. I had got rid of the poison that crippled all living things. People should not thank me for a murder which could only help to give the town a regrettable notoriety, but for a sacrifice. In addition, it would not be necessary to look for me further. I would never reveal myself.

You can get stamps and envelopes out of the automatic machines there. I stuck it down and was about to throw it in the box, but then I went to L. after all.

There was always a rabble hanging about in the main hall. The police weren't born yesterday, they might start asking questions, then someone would remember me. In L., if they ask, nobody will remember. And the journey only takes two hours. I like travelling by express at night, it is almost like a radio play, with the wheels thudding in a regular rhythm. I used to like listening to radio plays once upon a time. That was during the dull old days, but the feeling I got was pleasantly immediate. (It really would be wonderful if one could have the same feelings whilst one was writing as the others get from reading later on. But this way it is simply a bother.)

I heard the loudspeaker announcing the departure and hurried to platform six. Then bought a ticket from the guard. A moment of fright when he mentioned money, but I found more than enough in my pocket. It is such a long time since I thought about money.

On the way I read the newspaper again. It was only then that I noticed that the report contained useful information: the judge is not a judge at all, a pensioned off policeman from the vice squad, kicked out ten years ago because of misdemeanours. Used to go round with boy prostitutes—I suppose they mean the oily boys—and lived without any other social contacts. Many indications of kinky tastes in his flat.

I suddenly remembered my books. Now the coppers would be poking about in them. Still, what's done is done.

I've finished with all that.

Linz also has a post office by the station. But I put it in the outside posting box. So that nobody could be questioned. A chap in a grey overall came up behind me and emptied the box into a leather sack. There was a train back half an hour later. Perhaps my letter was travelling back with me in the same coach: the front half seemed to be a post section.

I almost forgot the goulash I had in the station buffet at Linz. Who knows what is really important in the progress of our lives? Perhaps later on it will emerge that the goulash was more important than the letter, on this trip to L. So I'll note it down.

After the goulash I bought a weekly. I didn't want to read any more about the judge, now that it was all done with. That subject is really finished with, I thought.

But then it turned out not to be finished, after all. I kept on tracing subtle connections running through so-called reality, which seem so unreal but are in fact more real than reality. The connection between my lofty thoughts on the subject of the judge and what I read in the weekly about the thieving singer, was striking. It almost took my breath away. However much I try to stand apart, in some mysterious way I am connected with the whole of mankind. I have this to say about the report on the woman singer:

The attraction of such reports is not so much in the facts that are given, but much more in the effect that these facts have on the reader. They renew one's awareness of the suppressed truth that nothing alive ever becomes fixed at a specified level. When, for example, it states that a singer who was once so famous and even today is well known, is wanted by the police, not only because she has avoided paying her debts, but because she has taken part in jewel thefts and break-ins, the reader thinks: by heaven, I didn't expect that!

For him the singer was a fixed institution, who for decades had been associated, in a strange irrational way, with the longing for travel, luxury and exotic eroticism. The Venezuelan nightingale awoke all these sweet longings with her popular songs and seemed—at least acoustically—to satisfy them at the same time. The anonymity of her voice coming through loudspeakers promoted the illusion that it came from beyond the tormentingly narrow limits of everyday reality. In the world from which this voice penetrated to us on earth, there seemed to be nothing but the romantic moon and the pure love which she sang about and which one could never enjoy because the archetypal purity of such values did not exist in reality. Here the individual thing seems to rule, never the concept.

The concept of 'Venezuelan nightingale' has a positive emotional value. It gives one a pleasant shock suddenly to rediscover it in an extremely negative connection. For years one had made an effort, which always remained inadequate, to make do with the painful present, to make a restricted, banal, and earthbound existence tolerable, by identifying— for the time it took to play a gramophone record—with the free, unearthly splendour on the other side. One admired the star that much more passionately, so that the identification would become even more satisfactory, more pleasant. But now that identification leaves behind the insipid after-taste which always clings to a substitute. It does not satisfy for long. Sooner or later it is followed by weariness and resignation, so that one enjoys a special relish if one suddenly has a chance to discover that the effort one made to identify was useless anyhow, because it had been wasted on an unworthy object. One had been quite wrong in making oneself unhappy at the thought that one would never enjoy great love under moonlit palm-trees, one had been wrong in thinking one's own life small in comparison to the great life of one's idol. Because this greatness has now been exposed as a hollow pretence, since the idol has sunk into the mire of crime. But we can find self-satisfaction in the steadiness and strength with which we have kept to the middle way of decency.

This is what I thought in the rolling train back from Linz, whilst I gazed at my shadowy face in the mirror of the dark compartment window. Only now and then fleeting buildings became visible in the light of arc-lamps behind the face.

People—I realised—live in a world of symbols and ideas. What they consider as facts are only their unconscious reaction to things that happen within themselves, and what they regard as active life is only a shadowy dance of death of their own feelings.

And yet, I told myself, I must take my trousers to a dry cleaner as soon as possible. An unreal event of the previous day had left ugly dark stains right up to the knees."

10

IN PASSING, I would like, as commentator, to draw the attention of the members of the commission to Zangl's strange blindness, his lack of contact, with himself too, because what he has to say about the passion people have for identification applies especially to him.

If it is possible for him to describe the feelings of the newspaper reader with regard to the singer who has become a criminal in such an ingenious way, why is it not possible for him to recognise his own feelings with regard to the judge or Dr. Kralicek? He shows a high degree of intelligence and intuitive insight when, on reading a murder report in a popular paper, he immediately grasps what the population wants in this kind of newspaper: it maintains a healthy balance between good and evil in the reader's consciousness, without burdening the conscience of the reader with the deed itself. The report of Zangl's murder is put alongside a report on the opening of a children's nursery. I got this particular edition of the paper out of the archives and can add to Zangl's reference by saying that this nursery had been built and paid for out of a public subscription, thus providing a symbol of good citizenship, which would reassure every reader as to how good and moral his society is.

Zangl, for his part, fulfilled his service to the community by providing a corpse as a balancing symbol of evil. Far be it from me to justify Zangl's act to the commission if I now point out that the society which did so much good for children also needed compensatory evil, without being able to admit to this need. This need for evil was satisfied by Zangl—it was latently present in the atmosphere and settled in Zangl for reasons which remain unknown, and it manifested itself through him in action.

I write: for reasons which remain unknown. Well, my report has shown us some of the prerequisites which made it possible for this evil to settle in Zangl, of all people. Just as my report has been able to suggest why Dr. Kralicek, of all people, with his house in a rose garden, with his profession, the white coat that he wore, with his interest in sick people obviously made it possible for Zangl to fixate on himself, on this particular doctor, his longings for a father figure, for a creator, for God, at the deepest level.

I mention the possibility of such relationships to make the commission consider whether society, in its striving for good, does not unwillingly create a need for evil, and with this need for evil, also put the executor of evil into the world, long before this executor becomes guilty as an individual.

With this exposition I have admittedly done more than consider Zangl as an isolated individual, without knowing whether I have met the wishes of the commission in so doing. So I shall return to the person of Zangl, in order to give a few more indications of the kind which will make it easier to understand the psychic development of Zangl.

Now that the commission has had an opportunity to become acquainted with my line of thought on more than one occasion, may I be allowed to sum up briefly: during the time we are able to see into Zangl's mind, the "low" or "dark" side of Zangl constantly strives for control of his conscious self. The "positive" side of Zangl desperately tries to defend itself, trying to counteract this dark force by intellectual means. Each time that the dark side takes a step forward and further isolates him from generally accepted thoughts and feelings, Zangl rebels with an act of violence. The first rebellion was the murder of the one in green, the second rebellion was the murder of the judge. Rebellion is followed by a period of apparent release. Zangl feels relieved and free to think "lofty" thoughts. This was his state immediately after Bernhard Leitner became his victim. But in spite of this feeling of release, the dark side in Zangl maintains its hold over him. Because the people he destroyed were not, as Zangl thought, the real evil, but only symbols of it. Should there happen to be an anthropologist on the commission, he would easily be able to explain to the other members of the commission that the kind of release from unknown forces through the representative killing of a symbolic figure, which we find in Zangl, is usual amongst primitive tribes.

At the deepest and most suppressed level of his mind Zangl knows the true state of affairs. The killing of symbolic beasts of sacrifice only give him a superficial release. In reality he is trying to draw the attention of society to his need through his actions.

I once called his murders "smoke signals for his rescuers". To enable these rescuers to track him down he leaves clues that point to him. He has to conceal these clues from his conscious mind, which is dominated by the dark side. So he leaves them for apparently logical reasons. He puts a slip of paper with his address in the book for the one in green; after the murder of the judge he writes letters to the newspapers and makes himself conspicuous by travelling to Linz with bloodstained trousers; he even eats some goulash there and draws the waiter's attention to himself by his improper behaviour. Should there be a criminologist on the commission, he would be able to report on similar phenomena to his colleagues, phenomena which are nothing new to the specialist engaged in the fight against crime: for example, the fact that faeces are sometimes left behind at the scene of the crime, or the obvious relief with which an apprehended criminal will make his confession to the authorities. Of course Zangl cannot admit these relationships to himself in the consciously formulated account of his behaviour which we find in his diary. So let us go on following the way in which he experiences himself and his conduct:

18th Evening

"Criminals—they say—are drawn to the scene of the crime. My desire to go to the funeral: is that what it is?

What a ridiculous question. To begin with I am not a criminal, secondly, the cemetery is not the scene of any crime.

Still, people could see it like that.

But if I don't go, it looks as though I am admitting that they are right.

That's what I thought, and I went. First I took the trousers to the cleaners. The woman behind the counter—but I don't want to waste time on such trivialities. One can't go into every little detail.

I walked slowly towards the gate. A good thing, that I did go slowly. If I'd gone quicker I would have stopped at the sight of the police car. But as it was I had time to overcome my impulse to pause.

(The more apathetically a man lives, the less he knows about himself, the more clearly he betrays his motives. I am wide awake. I do not hesitate. Perhaps it is for this reason, that I ponder such a lot, watch and observe myself: perhaps I really do not want to know myself all that much, but want to attain the ability to conceal my motives more effectively. Perhaps I also conceal them from myself?)

As I got nearer to the car I laughed at my own impulse. The two in the car were really quite harmless. They just sat there and stuffed themselves. Because drinking on the job is not allowed, but eating is.

They were two small, fat little men. I am sure they would have been afraid of officialdom. They didn't look a bit like agents of the penetrating voice of law and order. More like flat-footed watchmen who don't want to hear or see anything because their entire attention is focused on the food in the greaseproof paper. Their eyes have already divided the food into portions to be bitten off and swallowed, and their whole mechanism is adjusted to the business of biting off and swallowing. Anything else is a disturbance and a nuisance.

People who make such a fuss about death should pay a visit to the cemetery just once with their eyes wide open. With their eyes open, not veiled with tears and full of emotions. Looked at objectively the whole to-do is just theatre. You can see it quite clearly: the person left behind is always at the centre of all the fuss. Nobody really cares a fig for the corpse. If a person decks out a corpse with candles, satin, silver, flowers and organ music, it's only for himself. You can see from looking at the weeping widows that they made life hell for the dear departed. They were dissatisfied with him, with his income, with his habits, the way he smoked a pipe, did not wash his feet, drank beer in the bar. The moment he is dead he becomes the best of men. They bewail a lot of good qualities that he never possessed, relate a lot of good deeds that he never performed. They mourn a figure who never existed. And as they mourn, the figure comes to life at last. For too long reality has prevented the figure from coming to life, the real husband suppressed the one they dreamed of. But now, at last, he lives in the tears of contented widows, and deep down they are happy to have got their dream husbands at last. Which is why they spend a bit of money burying the deceased bastard.

The funeral parlour has six alcoves, in each of them there is a glass case like a refrigerated showcase, there is a coffin in each refrigerated trough. For expensive funerals the niche is draped with satin, and slender candles burn in a dignified manner beside the refrigerated shrine. The more respect a corpse enjoyed, the more flowers. If someone had no respect accorded to him at all you could buy him some here. Flowers and candles transform a simple corpse to a dear departed, silver and satin decorate the mortal remains.

The parlour is in use for nine hours every day, someone is disposed of every half-hour. Its ceremonial capacity is eighteen corpses per day. Accordingly the six alcoves are used three times per day, with a different corpse each time. Hardly has one been got out of the way, the place is cleaned up and the next one is displayed to the tearful gaze of the survivors. The corpse in alcove one comes off worst: it can only be laid out for half an hour, because the parlour is not opened until eight. At half-past eight the little electric bell up in the tower rings for the first time. The corpse in alcove six, on the other hand, which had also been laid out at eight, does not get its turn until eleven. Which is also the best time for a burial, because the participants, bowed down with grief, can go straight off for a meal together afterwards. Which is why alcove number six is the most expensive.

No wonder that the judge was in alcove number one, so that his turn came at half-past eight. No satin, no candles. All the same, he had been put in a coffin. But perhaps it was only hired. And there were no mourners, apart from the concierge and a gentleman in plain clothes, who looked like a policeman in disguise. Maybe a former colleague from the vice squad.

There was a much grander corpse in alcove two. There were flowers there, and sobbing women as early as quarter past eight. I stayed with them. As they came to fetch the judge the wandering choir began to sing in our grander alcove. It consists of six gentlemen who move from alcove to alcove all day—if they have been paid for—and sing. The rate of charges and the duration of the singing are precisely laid down. Ten minutes in this case.

If an alcove has not been paid for, the gentlemen betake

themselves to the cemetery restaurant and get up their strength with beer and sausages. They are therefore very well nourished, their necks immaculately shaved. You can see by the crushed state of the seats of their trousers that they own cars. It really is a fine profession: singer at funerals.

Not everybody is suited, because his manner must be both dignified, full of remote sympathy, and decisive, like that of a bailiff. Once they have finished their singing, for which they have blown themselves up like bullfrogs, they shrink back to normal size, give the chief mourners a sympathetic nod and move on ten yards to the next alcove with measured tread.

After them come less ceremonial figures. They are, after all, only public servants and not artists, namely, the pall-bearers. They wear black gowns and caps like lawyers in court. Only their leader is decked out with silver braid, like a public prosecutor. In his hand he carries a large key, from which dangles a rubber ball with the number of the refrigerated trough, like a hotel room key. After he has looked at a little card to check the contents of the trough, he unlocks it and nods to his minions. They pull out the coffin in a practised manner and press their shoulders under it. As they do this they turn their faces humbly to one side, so as to make room for the coffin on their shoulders. But people like to see it as a gesture of humility before inexorable death.

Then they either carry the coffin into a neighbouring hall, which is decorated with tasteful, if neutral frescoes—after all, corpses of all denominations are to be got rid of here, apart from Catholics, because this is where they cremate—or out to the open space in front of the chapel, where they load it on to a cart which is electrically driven and covered with satin. The cart, electrically powered and thus noiseless, then rolls slowly ahead of the mourners, whilst the pallbearers hurry on in front on a quicker cart. They get thrown out of their seats each time there is a bump in the ground, but this does not bother them, because they are used to it, and besides, they are allowed to smoke until they get to the grave.

The corpse from number two was cremated, and I followed the mourners into the frescoed hall. No expense had been spared : as the coffin came through the door heavenly organ music came out of loudspeakers covered with wax flowers. (Later I also discovered the slit in the ceiling through which the sound technician peers down so as to switch on the desired music at the right moment.)

The funeral industry in this town offers many nuances at different prices. They even have solemnities for corpses without a religion—a recitation. Alcove two had housed a corpse of this type, as I now discovered, for verses by Rilke suddenly rang out. Meanwhile the technician, from his lofty observation post, must have pressed yet another button, because some mysterious mechanism was set in motion, so that the coffin slowly sank into the ground. But the joints had apparently not been oiled for some time, because it creaked discreetly several times. Then the blossoms of the wreaths lying on the coffin trembled. Whilst intermittent sobs came from the front rows a gentleman next to me was telling his neighbour in a hissing undertone what was happening on the floor below. He said he knew exactly what was happening. He had been in Auschwitz.

As I was leaving an elderly gentleman with tears in his eyes spoke to me. Death, he said, kept on reminding us of the transience of life. Then he walked sadly away. I spent several more hours there, once I even followed the electric cart, because the fresh air, I noticed, did me good, and after standing for such a long time it was pleasant to stretch one's legs a bit between the graves.

As I left the cemetery I heard the bell toll, and even when I was on the tram I kept thinking of the sound engineer with his switchboard, whom most people confuse with fate.

After these notes I lay down on my bed and found that I was in high spirits.

Admittedly I was also full of sorrow. This mixture is as sweet and pleasant as the weariness which fills me after a day out in the open and so much physical movement. Perhaps I should go to funerals every day? But I haven't got time for that, since I need so much for thinking and writing.

I thought of my old flat, of the pit-pat of tennis balls, woven like pearls into the sound of the rising wind in the tree tops outside my window. Occasionally I heard a shrill whistle from far away, which reminded me of the school yard, of the hot dust of the ash track and the beating of my heart under the sweat-soaked shirt after the hundred-metre race. Then there was still space enough, and time. But here, in my room, there is only stifling closeness and the scraping of lodgers' feet in the staircase outside my window.

Oh Laurin, my Laurin, why did you forsake me?"

11

PERHAPS the voice of the commentator, with his endless explanations and asides, will already have got on the commission's nerves. All the same, I would like to draw attention to several things: the deeper Zangl sinks into mental confusion, the more often he mentions God in his comments. No doubt the layman acquainted with depth psychology has been aware for some time that there is a deep and meaningful connection between Zangl's unconscious longing for a father, his compulsive need to force Dr. Kralicek into the role of a magician, his question about the recognisability of God in the flow of the canal, between all these things, a connection we can only guess at, in spite of all possible explanations. Zangl's memory of his nocturnal childhood experience, when he hid himself under the blanket and still feared that God might take this game of hide-and-seek as an offence, is related to Zangl's anxiety in case the doctor should blame him for trying to go behind his back. I am only mentioning these relationships here as a pointer, and refrain from commenting at length, for instance, on Zangl's exclamation: "Laurin, Laurin, why have you forsaken me?" which he notes down just at a point when he believes time and space to be lost forever.

The commission might consider whether questions about moral responsibility are necessary in the case of Zangl, since our material lacks all evidence for the existence of a spiritual voice for the creation of a morality—it lacks any indication of a belief in the necessity of society, of a belief in God or any other absolute.

Now, since all searching proved to him to be in vain, Zangl moved inexorably towards his own goal. In the dream which makes up his next entry in the diary he at last establishes the absence of God as an unalterable fact, so that finally, but not before (just like the frightened child under the blanket shook his fists at the cold eye) he has diverted his rage to the direction where God lives, or does not live, namely, against the doctor. Then Zangl says good-bye to this world, which he no longer thinks it worthwhile to inhabit, since it did not come to his help and was so little able to understand the tracks that he had left behind him, just as he could not understand himself.

His diary says:

Morning
"I saw God's feet in my dream. They were bandaged, like those of a mummy, and God lay on a catafalque, at the bottom of a deep pit. In the dream I had a limited field of vision, as though I was looking through a keyhole. Saw, as I said, only a patch of stone floor, a stone wall in the background, the whole thing flooded with dusty, stony light. God seemed to have been resting here for a fixed eternity, in this Gothic dungeon. At the foot of the catafalque I spotted a sculpture in grey granite: it depicted a winged figure which, with the help of its wings, was lowering itself on to its own deathbed. Underneath was written, in old-fashioned script '. . . here lyeth, thus awfully layd to rest . . .'

As I read it, it was quite clear to me, even in the dream, that this room of death concealed a ghastly secret. The *mise-en-scène* and the inscription were supposed to give the onlooker an impression that the dead person had laid himself down to an eternal rest here of his own free will and under his own steam. But in actual fact he had simply been thrown down from above. The artist, who had made the inscription, knew about it, but followed the order of his own day and gave the figure wings. He chose the word 'awfully', which during that long gone period must have had more the meaning of 'inspiring awe' in common speech, in order to indicate, together with the wings, that not merely a dead God, but one killed in his fall lay here. The deep understanding of an artist of a pre-intellectual era, who did not want to betray his knowledge completely.

I too am a seeker after truth!

When I had my talks with Laurin I never thought of it, but now it suddenly occurred to me, quite spontaneously, the story of my childish dialogue with God. With Laurin, when I referred to 'God', I thought more of the official image, that the skinny woman painted for me, or of my momentary vague feeling of something 'flowing', of an 'All' or 'Nothing'. Because I had my first contact with the problem of God much earlier, when I was little, and made use of the Almighty every night so as not to wet the bed. (I wet the bed and was beaten for it. I also adopted, unquestioningly, the opinion of the outside world on the subject of bedwetting—it was shameful. I wanted deliverance.)

Whenever the light was switched off and I was ordered to go to sleep, I thought of the apparently unavoidable disgrace of the oncoming night. Then I remembered the Almighty, whom I never thought of otherwise, and turned to him with the plea that he might rescue me from the sin of piddling. But at the same time I despised myself for only drawing near to the highest court of appeal, which I found so difficult to visualise, when I wanted something for myself, whilst I never gave it a thought at other times. If this highest court of appeal really existed—on the subject of which I did not dare to form an opinion—it would consider this self-seeking to be punishable.

Self-seeking prayers are undoubtedly not granted.

So I would immediately pray to God, asking him to forgive me for being self-seeking. And in order to wipe out the disadvantageous impression of self-seeking I tagged on to my prayer a request for the well-being of other people. I regarded my own behaviour as a mean and shabby trick, the kind practised by horsedealers, and therefore prayed that my peasant cunning might be overlooked. But I only asked so that my first prayer might have a better chance of being granted. So that my prayer for forgiveness on account of my peasant cunning was in itself peasant cunning ...

In this way I heaped sin upon sin before going to sleep, always in the hope that God would grant me control. But God remained silent. The only sound in the child's room was the ghostly cracking noise in the cupboard, which was inhabited by spirits and witches. So, still praying, I ducked under the blanket, into fearful dreams. Mostly I then turned to face the gaze of a rigid eye, which was constantly directed towards me and which—even if one shook one's fist up at it and spat or bellowed rude words—continued to be unassailable and motionless.

In the corner of a building site I repeated the situation: I, or more precisely, the strange child that I once was, caught an ant and held a lens above the animal, motionless, rigid, deadly. The child played 'Eye of God'. The child that I think about in my room, is that supposed to have been me once? I can scarcely believe it. In any case, I am full of pity.

I myself, that is true, am full of dark shadows. But the child I remember is something so clear, so clean and round. Who could find the heart to place it in a situation in which it is surrounded on all sides with invisible opportunities to become guilty, so that it always lives in the constant expectation of unpredictable punishment? If I could find him—oh, how I would hate him! How I would punish him for his atrocity!

Lay on the bed and thought, while the butts accumulated

on the floor. Thought about God and the cold eye, from which no mercy came.

The child did not really repent, did not really lay himself open and abandon himself with proffered throat, the way I gave myself to Laurin, there on his couch. He simply added to the chain of purposeful assurances. At the bottom of his soul he retained his silent reservation, doubt and the purpose too!

But could he have done otherwise?

He had been told about this highest court of appeal. Trustingly he turned to it, though admittedly he was vague about the address, but the court did not answer.

Perhaps it was a false address? Perhaps I found myself on the throne, when they said God sat on it? Perhaps this was the reason why I, in my capacity as my God, kept rejecting myself in my capacity as a child, filling myself with fear and trembling?

Perhaps the operation came to grief because of an unwillingness to have faults. The child wished to be free of sin and to do everything to avoid guilt. I am guilty of wanting to be guiltless.

I don't want to be caught out, no!

Why did that stupid idiot at the dry cleaner's keep asking me for my name? Surely it can't matter to her. Do I have to leave my visiting card behind, wherever I go, just because I happen to own a pair of dirty trousers?

And if it really is the custom to write customers' names in a little book at cleaners, it's still a scandal. Well, in the end they took them without my giving it.

Now I'm going to buy some rolls and smoked sausage.

Only when I ride off to intellectual heights on my thoughts, the way Nils Holgerson rode on the back of a goose, do I forget that vague tormenting feeling that I'm living under a pane of frosted glass. Somehow I have the suspicion that, unknown to me, something is developing which directly concerns me. Only I can't make it out. Then I feel betrayed and shamefully misused. Then I am the unsuspecting child that the seeing eye allows to stumble into sin and guilt without a scruple.

Whilst I wander about cluelessly in the bizarre landscape of my thoughts like a terrarium of skilfully disguised plaster, in which nothing changes and time makes no difference, outside this abode a clockwork mechanism goes on: the time-fuse ticks.

I feel something like this, for example, if I now compare, in a musing fashion, the changing conditions in which I have been and now am: it seems to me as though this organism, which believes itself to be me, is nothing more than an uninteresting mechanism being controlled now by this, now by that. Like a hire car which is used by drivers at their convenience and does not see or know its drivers.

So nothing happens because one wants it to. This stops me, now that I recognise the situation, from happily saying 'yes' to myself, the way other people do, and the way I used to myself in the old days. On the other hand I don't have to care a damn if the odd person falls victim to me. The ultimate guilt does not lie with me, but with the driver.

Just read a comment on Socrates in the *Reader's Digest*. A worthwhile magazine. You get more for your money than you do with other magazines. And anything that is worthwhile spurs me on to thinking. Anything that spurs me on to thinking is worthwhile. At least, for me. I found out to my joy that I am Socrates. Because I too cry out to myself: Know thyself. (That is, my driver, who steers me.)

And like Socrates, I say that I know nothing. That I do not know my driver.

I know I am at one with Socrates, not with his disciples. Because it is only the disciples who are overbearing and criticise others for falsely believing that they know anything. But this is just the fault that the master reprimands: to believe that one knows anything—even if it is only the knowledge that one knows nothing. The difference is minimal but yet so significant. The master says:

'I know that I know *nothing*!'

But the false disciples yell in a chorus:

'*I know* that I know nothing!'

Only the individual, all on his own, ever succeeds in knowing that he knows nothing. The group never succeeds in being wise.

And I am supposed to fit in with a group?

What for, I ask? Just to be another greedy consumer in the collective?

What for, I ask?

A man thinks he lives within his thoughts. But this is not true. He lives independently of his thoughts, and thinking has nothing to do with 'life'. An animal has no doubts, and yet it lives. And it is, although it does not know it. So life is something that can never be grasped through thinking, because it exists prior to thinking, more than that, it is a prerequisite.

But who lives me, who is my prerequisite, who gives me my thoughts?

A plan, the magnitude of which intoxicates me! At last I have found the way that leads to myself. It is so simple, yet was so hard to find.

Tomorrow I shall go at once in search of my thoughts. If it is as Laurin says, and as I myself believe, then all my thoughts, all my feelings have been in the world long before me and have been thought and felt by other people. I only have to go to the national library and look for them there amongst the book backs. I'll collect them together like the pieces of a puzzle. I shall fit them together—and get myself!

God, I'm so happy!

But it's a pity that it is Sunday tomorrow. I'm sure it won't be open then.

Monday morning: the beginning of a new life. How strong I feel, how fresh!

Before I set off, made a quick entry about yesterday: stuck the newspaper reports about the judge in *My Fight*. I didn't even read all of them, the contents could hardly hold my attention any more. I found the report of the disaster in the pit much more gripping.

(Since I saw God lying there pits mean something special to me.) How illogical human beings are: one thanks the 'rescuers', who really don't deserve having been given the opportunity to do great deeds. They were only doing their duty. Mr. XYZ, who perhaps might have shown a much greater greatness, if he had had the opportunity, has to make do with longing for a greener flat.

It is not the 'rescuers' who deserve our thanks, but those who, as the tools of destiny, first provided the prerequisites which gave the rescuers something to rescue—it is to them that the rescuers owe their thanks, I mean those who built the pool so badly that the water ran into the pit. Now they berate them as 'guilty'. But it is not only them they forget to thank, but those others who, without having a clue, just because they like to make trouble, obstinately maintained that there were people still alive down there. The rescuers go down only to squash these rumours, so that they received thanks and awards for nothing more than their petty desire to teach rumour-mongers a lesson.

I also came across a review of Steinbeck: I really must read this chap some time (now I'm sorry about the loss of the library, because I seem to have given myself away in giving it away), because his name makes me think of the back of a rock, sticking out of the mossy ground like a white elephant. And out of the wrinkles grow little grasses whose milky white blossoms blow in the wind like bells summoning the gnats to church.

I am sure he has written beautiful books, full of the heat of the sun and the quiet of noon.

If I still had the shop, I'd have gone straight there yesterday, to look for Steinbeck. Or I wouldn't have minded going to the national library, except that they were closed for Sunday. Sanctity of an arbitrary day maintained by police regulation: how hollow this world is, and only a scarred, cracked crust of police regulations arches like a dead skin over a long dead blister, which burst without anyone noticing it. There are only dogmas left, but not a sign of life anywhere.

So I wasted yesterday, when I could have made use of it in my drive towards knowledge, if the librarians had been on duty. Instead I lay flat on my back and thought about eating smoked sausage and made the modest discovery that I only liked smoked sausage so much because in a previous existence I would like to have been one of the woodcutters who axed the lime tree in granny's garden. (They sat on the trunk and ate their sausage, and the air was full of the scent of the wood, of beer and men's sweat and distant monkey calls, whilst granny was looking for me all over the house.)

This note-taking is like a dangerous game with a boomerang: I fling out my words but they come back to me like huge black birds and gobble me up.

(For example, I would now like to follow the allegory of words and semen in all its ramifications: the words are my semen, and they come back to me as children who swallow up their father. Perhaps I would also have destroyed my father, had I known him . . . But I must go now! I'm going! Right away, or my words will swallow me up completely.)"

12

I AM BRIEFLY interrupting Zangl's manuscript here to point out how aggression is once more building up inside him, unknown to himself. We recall his cry of long ago against that power which knowingly allowed an ignorant child to stumble into guilt: If I could find him—oh, how I would hate him! And we recall the connection I pointed out between father, God, Dr. Kralicek and Zangl himself, which —as I informed the commission earlier—was projected on to the person of the doctor in a way which was becoming dangerous for him. Therefore a terrible threat lies in those apparently harmless words: perhaps I would also have destroyed my father. We know the process whereby the consciousness of Zangl always fills up with reflections on cultural philosophy and literary history when deep disturbances are taking place in his subconscious. The consequence of such disturbances is always a new distribution of the roles that Zangl wishes to ascribe to the people around him. In the final conclusion which Zangl always draws from his apparently objective consideration of heroism, the Emperor of China, the allegorical connection between words and semen, or whatever, we always find—distorted, it is true, but recognisable now to our experienced eyes—the shadowy contours of his inner, real attitude. What is it, for instance, that Zangl finds so gripping about the theme of the Chinese Emperor's conversion? Nothing other than the question, what determines a human being's individuality: the specific structure of his consciousness in so far as it can be formulated in ideas, or

the identity of his body, which remains unaltered throughout the course of his life? For Zangl, himself subject to a
powerful division of consciousness, this question is of vital
significance. At first the question arises in his mind in a way
that appears to have nothing to do with himself, but in the
course of development it then becomes more and more personal, always applied more directly to himself and finally
expresses itself in the idea that he himself—Xaver Ykdrasil
Zangl—resembled a hire car being driven by a total stranger.
The question of a person's identity is not one being asked by
Zangl alone, since heart transplants started and people are
getting ready to transplant brains: the heart is only a muscle,
and a person's identity, in so far as we see this as anchored
in his consciousness, is not affected by transplanting this
lump of flesh. But if the brain of a murderer, his memories
and thoughts, in short, his entire consciousness is trans-
planted into the head of a stranger, then the question arises,
which now has the identity of the murderer: the lifeless
hand, which committed the murder, or the nervous system
which guided the hand?

I am drawing attention to this fact, the close connection
between apparently objective reflections and Zangl's subjective and compulsive ideas, because I can see in advance
that some of the members of the commission will accuse me
of overloading my report with too many lengthy quotations
from Zangl's diary. I can just hear one or other of the commission's members saying formally: "Although these literary
and historical discussions are quite interesting in parts they
have nothing to do with Zangl's sexual murders, they belong
in a literary magazine but not between the slaughter of the
victim and dessert." Now, it really belongs in an inseparable
fashion to the slaughter of the victim, if the commission
wishes to get as full as possible a picture of Zangl, who only
appears to be an isolated case. For this reason I cannot spare
the commission from having to read more of Zangl's philo-

sophising—but if the commission approaches it with a willingness to understand, they will gain by it, whatever questions were uppermost in their minds.

Saturday

"My stomach swollen, almost dizzy with lack of blood to the brain, at the desk. I must force myself to work at something real. The only tangible reality at the moment: this sentence. How pathetic! What a dreadful time, these past twelve days! The whole time in the periodical room. (They want an identity card in the reading room. This scared me off, I don't know why.) Read and read, lost myself completely in the process. Everything is true, everything is false. Everything belongs to me, nothing belongs to me. I kept finding myself all over the place, but only in fragments. A bit here, a bit there. I am not in a position to fit myself together. It is worse than before.

I can just remember one sentence which I agreed with enthusiastically, until I noticed how false it is. Friedell is supposed to have said: 'What we call events are basically, especially where creative people are concerned, nothing but projections of the personality extended to the outside world, characteristics flowing into facts.' How true, I thought at first. But then it occurred to me: this would mean, as far as I am concerned, that my character consisted of murder and killing.

Everything in me defends itself against this idea: that can't be! But it is made easy for me to believe it, because—being proud of representing the signs of the times in their purest form—I read in an essay: 'The total relativisation of all the normalities of our lives has taken on Einsteinian proportions during the last forty years, the chaos of murder and reason can no longer be contained with the benevolent detachment of a Thomas Mann.'

(Now that I've persuaded myself to write after all, I already

G

feel better. The anger I felt towards the author also drove
me on : how can he give such a well-phrased lecture on the
chaos of murder and reason without his throat being choked
with helpless, raging agony? Anyone who does not stammer
incomprehensibly on this subject is lying.)

If he were right, then the judge would be nothing but the
chaos of murder and reason in my character spilling over
into fact. How can he condemn me to such a role?

If I hoped to find my face in the national library, the
opposite occurred : that is where I lost it once and for all.
For example, I once wrote that I was for the socialists. What
a mistake, as Weizsäcker teaches me : After them, human
beings today are only left with the choice between death and
an existence as small cogs in a big machine, which alone
permits our continuing existence, since it doles out bread
and love according to plan.

Yes, faced with this future my heart beats only for the
right-winged worm in the roots of the west, who is for a
classless village school and who dreams of the soil at night,
for this apparent wretch is fighting on my behalf, for the
unorientated human being, because he is already opposing
those laws, which are, even now, inexorably at work to adapt
and integrate us into the collective. As Canetti says, the
much deeper, and the real, impetus of history is the drive of
humanity to become part of a higher animal species, the
crowd, and to lose itself totally within it.

I protest against this statement. No, no, I do not want to
be part of the crowd. I don't want to go into this darkness,
in which there is no more escape from the eye. It's shocking
to write stuff like that. Is there no censorship? I suddenly
turn rigid at the sentence I have just written : I am calling
for censorship, me, after writing to the Bishop of Limburg
only a little while back? (And suddenly I remember : didn't

I note down the demand, that authors should write only homogeneous material?

Homo genius?)

But here, in the periodical room, I also called for censorship once, when I read the obituary for Ossietzky. What boundless liberalism, that spreads out and wants to get us up out of our holes—those devils, who would throw me on the rubbish heap of history right away. Editors who print such stuff should be sent to prison, before I go soft and order a Jewish badge, a club tie and cuff-links shaped like trumpets, to be the vassal of those gentlemen in Cologne. Where they are concerned I am absolutely on the bishop's side.

Then I come across an old acquaintance, my friend Jung. And now I am on his side in thinking that—an idea which all the old mystics had too—God is the intangible All which also signifies nothing, and which consists of the sum of all contradictions, which cancel each other out. Then man, in so far as he can understand himself through thinking— and he only is in so far as he can—has been constructed out of single parts torn up from the All-Nothing. So man is a part of God, but by nature the opposite of God, because he came into being through limitation, whilst God exists through expansion. I keep screaming that I don't want to be adapted, and in doing so I am screaming in the name of the freedom of my self (without knowing what that self is). Having now said all this, if I again ask myself what use a man should make of his freedom, then I would now have to say, that a man should use his freedom to select those areas in which he wants to give up his freedom. Because only in this way can he become more and more human. So freedom consists in giving up freedom: so the Communists are right in their assertion that freedom is understanding necessity, and I am a Communist! That's what you get when you consciously try to know yourself, and I am in total agreement with an essay which shows that the excessive value we put on awareness is the curse of our time, because it destroys the balance between reasoned and instinctive behaviour.

In the next issue of the periodical someone gives an answer after my own heart with the comment: This balance was destroyed long ago through the one-sided stress of civilisation, in that it broadened the area of freedoms to an indigestible extent, so that man was robbed of his feel for life, which only arises out of a sense of obstacles. What possibilities still existed, which a human being could imagine but not realise? (The author asks this. But I scribble the following sentence in the margin of the periodical: Remote control by long distance radio signals is enough to send me to hell and back.) What a mistake to think that the world has got bigger through prosperity and air traffic! On the contrary! In the minds of human beings it has shrunk to the size of a provincial town. So I am, if I follow my train of thought, among the most extreme of reactionaries, in wanting a limitation on freedoms. So I go round aimlessly in a circle, in the course of a single afternoon twist round on my arse one and a half times.

I cannot even hold on to this as my personality, what I thought for a moment I had found under the name Musil: the fact that I am a Man without Qualities. Because I have got qualities, they just don't happen to be mine. Even the quality of not going anywhere doesn't come from me, shines out at me from an essay by Pascal, if I read:

1. The people's belief in the state is based on truth
2. this truth is a fiction and hence no truth
3. the belief, since untrue, is justified as belief
4. since it is justified, it becomes truth.

A handful of brain cells create an entire cosmos out of nothingness!

Not only are my thoughts not *my* thoughts—my feelings

don't belong to me either. If I wanted to swing a whip over
the one in green from behind a screen, the pleasure this gave
me was borrowed from the Marquis de Sade. And if, my
pulse racing, I pressed my ear against the wall, the idea
came from Cendrars—such richness in his work: he can
permit himself to dispose of the events of an entire year in
one aside. It is a horrible experience, suddenly to find oneself
in an intimate hall of mirrors, when one believed oneself to be
in the humming market place. The humming is only the
sound of one's own blood and the breadth of the square is
conditioned by the closeness of the mirrors.

And out of one of these mirrors steps a part of my assumed
self in the mask of Jean Genet, or rather, in the mask of his
characters—and I recognise the judge. (How much still
slumbers concealed in me, in relation to the judge? I turn
away in fear.)

Leiris and Bataille, Cioran, Sartre, Camus and a man called
Havemann: out of dusty bundles of paper bearing these
names a face looks out at me, which I took to be my own.

If I wanted to describe myself, it would be enough to write
a sort of index, in this fashion: 'Henry James, Penguin
Classics 1919, p. 8', in order to reproduce a component of
myself. So one of my opinions, which until now I always
regarded as *my* view, because it came to me in the still hours
of meditation, is described by Henry Miller: the world, a
senseless affair, in which some unknown power keeps inter-
fering. And fear men's chief drive. They are clay in the
hands of the fearless, just as the judge was ultimately putty
in my hands.

(Now I ask myself whether it would not have been better
to make more than just a corpse out of it.)

Wandering hopelessly in this ghostly landscape of dead
ideas, which have sucked on to me like leeches, so as to
borrow a little life from me, one sentence fills me with hope
for seconds: 'We will not free ourselves of this fear by ceas-

ing to go round in mental circles, but by abandoning ourselves to something worthwhile.' Yes, I want to abandon
myself, to something!

But to what? I suddenly ask myself. It is to find out just
this that I have to let my thoughts go round in circles.
Even these words of wisdom reveal themselves as an empty
husk . . .

Lay on my bed for hours, exhausted. Did not feel the cold.
It all seems so senseless.

I suppose I am rotten at the core. Like an apple, I've been
treated chemically with gnosticism and agnosticism, idealism
and pragmatism, Catholicism and Calvinism, socialism, com-
munism, psychologism, egocentrism—and this treatment has
blown me up like a balloon. If I had been left untreated—
who knows, I might have remained an unsightly, mis-shapen
but healthy apple. But as it is my skin is splitting from all
the chemicals injected into me, and like maggots the most
various opinions worm their way through my tormented
flesh. Nothing is firm. Nothing lasts. Like the words: they
sit loose and askew like alien feathers in a mangy fur, and
when I want to catch hold of myself nothing is left in my
hand but a sticky bit of stinking language.

Yes, this is how the matter must stand: since man is
defined through his capacity to know and this is defined as
being incomplete, every tangible truth is a bad one, because
it is an incomplete truth. It may be clear, but it is not quite
true. Because the truest truth is an unclear truth. But it is
pointless to express this, because it expresses nothing. It says
everything—and nothing. Neurotics like me have crawled
right down to the mothers inside ourselves and we still want
to talk about it. But madmen go further: they have crawled
right down to the crowd inside themselves and have lost
themselves in the process, have dissolved into Canetti's higher

animal species. They already live there, where everything is trodden down, each voice is heard. Only madmen, who can no longer say anything, are in possession of the real, the full truth. People like us, who still have the desire to speak, always have to make do with half of it. It would be a step forward to give up this wish. One should become mad in order to achieve fullness, nothingness. Because I lose all courage when I see how many tacit assumptions I have to make in order to be able to begin to speak at all.

Full moon night. Werewolf night. I dreamt a new discovery: the God in the pit was me.

I climb through the shadows that the moon throws into my room via the staircase, as though they were the stiff branches of a petrified forest. My body is swollen up and fluorescent like the body of a magic corpse. I am afraid of the strange cry of fear that someone would let out if they saw me like this. In the black concealment of my bed an idea comes into my mind with sudden clarity, and I realise with a shudder that in the darkness of prehistory life spilled over from expression to self-expression: this was the moment when mankind was born. Because an animal is lived, but a man lives himself. Only I myself do not exist. Am not a man, not an animal. I am a paper index in the secret drawer of Laurin's desk: HE fashioned me out of ideas!

Another day

Daylight, even if it only penetrates the staircase and the frosted glass of my window in a muted form, makes the problems seem less agitating than this spooky white moon. And the horrifying truth also seems more bearable during the day.

It is a matter of learning to live with the fact that I do not exist. How absurd it sounds: I do not exist.

But it is true. Only my animal side, my drive to get food and sleep, and to get rid of my semen, of course, only this could perhaps be recognised as my personal being. Everything over and above that, ideas, the language I speak, yes, even the forms in which the animal drives express themselves, are alien products, have been dictated to me by Laurin from his index. (I remember a line that Musil must have written once: 'Inexpressible, dull misery: cannot write!' Well, the times Laurin demanded this condition of me—over and over again!)

When this influence of Laurin's began, I don't know. But no doubt it has existed since the first time I went to see him.

I've just been working it out: that was sixty-seven days ago.

Looking back, I am surprised at my own blindness. Why didn't I notice it sooner?

At the beginning, when I used to gaze up at him enthusiastically and wanted nothing better than to be allowed to sit at his feet for an unending dialogue, that must have been the time he found most agreeable. He got his money on the dot. I was a sort of accumulator: he charged me a bit and then got as much as he could out of me.

But something must have gone wrong with his calculations. I got away from him, made myself independent, began to go my own way. The image I have of myself is very apt: I am a hire car with broken steering.

Laurin sensed what was happening. Cautiously he fished for information. The scales fell from my eyes when he looked at me with that strange look and said to himself: 'Very interesting, your fantastic remoteness.' He wanted to find out how much I might already know. He was laughing at me all the time.

Laurin, I know it now, is the merciless eye! Clear realisation pours over me like a waterfall. Suddenly everything fits together: Laurin's affable manner at the beginning, then his sharpness when I threatened to slip out of his grasp. Yes, the one in green too: he must have hated her for some reason or other, so that I had to kill her as his instrument! Like a pianist he tuned me to murder and sent me on my way.

Only as far as the judge is concerned, maybe it was not like that.

There something went wrong for the magician. But what does he care. Perhaps the judge was also one of his minions. (In fact, I'm pretty sure of it.) Perhaps he felt sorry for the old gossip.

It's a good thing I did not give him the Black Book. Because he only asked for it to see how much I had found out about him . . .

Lay on the bed. Whenever I am resting I become particularly receptive to Laurin's attempts to establish contact.

The apparent spontaneity of my actions and thoughts is always due to Laurin. He is on the defensive. Tries to sow the seeds of doubt.

I thought spontaneously that my last discoveries could be a wicked trick of some complex or other, designed to trap me. I now mistrust all my discoveries. Perhaps they are all a shadow play put on by Laurin, in order to deceive me.

('Me'—which of my selves is speaking? The self which is Laurin's slave, it undoubtedly is not. Somewhere or other there really must be the remainder of a real, personal self, concerned with the pressing desire to become myself. A brave little band.)

I should not lie here. Obvious, that the eternal Jew has to wander:

Anything persistent immediately detaches itself.

One must be courageous. I'm in a vast battle which, some-how or other, is coming to a climax. In this state one must reckon with anything and keep one's eyes open. Courageously I must bear in mind that everything is justified: my doubt and my doubt about my doubt.

So has Laurin made me or not? If he had not made me and I still existed—what then? Then my conviction that he has made me would be the voice of a gnawing darkness inside me, that wishes me harm.

Then I would have killed the one in green and the judge out of an evil impulse which only seemed to be well-founded. In that case I should go over to Laurin as fast as possible, as he himself advised me to once. ('But if it overwhelms you, then you just ring me up, do you hear? Day or night. We don't want anything bad to happen!')

Shall I call him? The idea is very tempting. Would it be weakness, if I followed it?

But what would be the sense of confessing everything quite openly to Laurin? To tell him that my basic weakness is a fear of life, to tell him that I killed the one in green because in my dealings with her I could not assert myself fully, since I do not exist?

Am I supposed to tell him that, when he has known all this for ages, since he made me? Him, who made me just this way so that he could *misuse me as his representative?*

How despicable he is, to humiliate me into the bargain by letting me believe that I let him create thoughts for me, when in actual fact it is I who am living for him! I must not think any more at all, I must not show him my weak side. I shall go out. He won't get at me so easily out in the street.

After Midnight

The ghosts of the night? No full moon today, just blackness and fear. In the black, unending ocean the cone of light from my lamp is the only protection which remained to me. I sit in it as though in a diver's bell. In it I fled from sleep, from this dreadful dream. The only way in which I can still exist: writing.

On my way through the streets—yes, a mysterious power once more drew me to colonies of toadstools. All this filth inside me . . . It was my dream that first showed me that it really does come from Laurin. Because the thoughts he has planted in me were supposed to make me blind to the way my senses were going on his behalf. Laurin had once more sent me out on to the streets in order to kill! Yes, I would like to have spoken to one of the toadstool colony, and I know where that leads. Then I thought: no, better go to Laurin. I said to myself: tell him everything, see how he reacts. If he looks as though he has been caught out, free yourself from him. I even bought myself a knife—for all eventualities.

What a madman he is. Every twenty-two days he gets a lust for blood, then I have to go out and get it for him. The first day I went to him he killed me and filled me up with his material, without my noticing anything: didn't I tell him that I wouldn't be talked into his God—and now I have fantasies about God all the time? Since then I have been walking around like a dead man. In the West Indies they know a form of magic for using the dead as a cheap labour force. I am a West Indian corpse, getting reinforcements for Laurin's penal colony: twenty-two days after my own death, the one in green. She'll be running round like a zombie now, as well. How can I save myself? Who could give me a convincing way out? The judge died twenty-two days after the one in green. And yesterday, as I described my nocturnal feeling with the words 'Full moon night. Werewolf night'— *it was once more twenty-two days since the judge died!*

Laurin is a vampire, he has made me into a vampire! I must

calm down, write it down clearly, in order to get my mind under control.

I did not speak to anyone in the toadstool colony, nor did I go to the rose garden, because while I was skirting round the toadstool colony I suddenly saw Laurin! He was coming out of the cinema by the station. They are showing the French film *The Devils*. I immediately thought that he was only using the cinema as a hiding place, so that he could steer me more effectively from close quarters, unobserved. I thought this right away. But I also thought that I could get away from his influence. The realisation that the miserable images of lust in my head were not my own at all drove them away like shadowy ghosts.

But then I dreamt: the judge and the one in green were married. Whilst the one in green is away, shopping, the flowerpot stand falls on the judge's head. The judge is dead. Suddenly I am out in the street and see the one in green with her patent leather bag, carrots are sticking out of it, going under a huge runaway horse. She is pushed over and dragged along, then she lies still and is dead. Then I am in a bathroom. It is time for the one in green to come home from the shops, but she is dead. I saw her die myself. Then suddenly, the corpse of the judge rises up with a gurgling noise from the greenish, foaming water in the bath. The shock quite cripples me. But he doesn't even see me. He goes to the door and opens it. Outside stands the one in green and comes in, straight towards me ...

I got up with a scream and fled here, under the light by the table.

It is obvious to me: Laurin is even making my dreams! (The scene in the bathroom: it just so happens that I know this bit—I saw *The Devils* a long time ago. In a flash I also realise why I was able to believe, for a time, that my dreams were good film material: they always were film material, long before Laurin let me dream them! How can I ever escape from him? Laurin has made me. He is my father. He is the eye into which I have to spit. Spontaneously I think: I shall kill him, in order to free myself at long last.)"

13

XAVER YKDRASIL ZANGL did not kill Dr. Kralicek. In this strange mixture of madness and insight, which we have had sufficient opportunity to examine thoroughly, he also constructs himself a reason for *not* being allowed to kill, just as before he had already, on two occasions, made out reasons why he *should* kill. In his last diary entry, he writes:

"Before I step across into the great, timeless oneness, in which going and standing still become one, like speaking and silence, waking and sleeping, hope and fear, light and darkness—before I step over into the unspeakable nothingness, I have this to add:

In the beginning was the word. And the word was Laurin. And it created me and made me into his creature, in all that I did, thought and felt. At the finish he even wanted to kill himself through my hands, so that he would know that I would then have to wander alone over the face of the earth, lost and forsaken. But I will not allow him that devilish pleasure.

He commanded me to wander high and low, and feasted on the pain that the separation caused me, by which I was born through the power of the word. He even drove me towards the abyss, watched by the mocking, silent eye. It was only when I looked in the mirror that I recognised the horror in its totality: at the newspaper kiosk, when I wanted to buy cigarettes in the drizzling rain of this grey day, this last of days.

'The Fugitive Murderer' screamed the colourful headline under the picture of a being, that I had always believed to be *me*.

The story of this person is oddly familiar and yet so strange, like that of a double I met in a dream. But it is not a dream—this mound of realities, things and facts that this double has piled up round me, in Laurin's service, whilst my eyes were directed totally on spiritual things, so as to catch sight of myself through the fog, not suspecting that I, who directed my gaze, *am not*, just as what I was looking at *is not*.

Behind my back the trap has been set up, the trap with which they want to try and pull me into the narrow and terribly banal world of trivial realities, the world of bite-and-swallowers, wearers of clothes, left- and right-wing orators, turnkeys, guards, institute overalls and other zombies, who imagine themselves safely in a reality which is nothing but pure invention.

A logical consequence and a compelling conclusion reveal themselves to my horrified eyes, when I now look back under the projecting roof of the newspaper kiosk: I hold the paper in my hands as though it was a sieve, and like someone washing for gold I find in it, distorted into bizarre shapes, 'facts', which I was unable to recognise in the stream of intangible time.

In the 'reality' of this newspaper report, which was never mine and yet somehow looks like mine now, people who are decisive make their appearance—although I scarcely noticed them. It almost seems to me as though they were made up afterwards: post office officials and waiters, hotel porters, railway porters, pedalling apes. Everybody is trying to force me to become identical with my vain, dirty double, I am being surrounded, there is no way out. They don't intend that anything of me, the lofty one, should remain.

Laurin wishes this out of revenge, because I did not kill

him, refused to carry out his command. He too is in the picture puzzle which the newspaper describes as though it was my real life: although he stays in the background he makes a brief appearance at the edge of the picture as the private physician of the dead judge.

But I am robbed of the possibility of becoming a thing that I can catch hold of myself, because everything about me that is concrete, my actions as well as my motives, belong to my double: the creature that Laurin made.

Whilst I walked from the kiosk back to my diver's bell through the grey rain, I found the solution I had been searching for so long:

I can escape from Laurin and become completely myself by giving up my consciousness, which chops up the wholeness of things and makes two different things out of the real Good-Evil. I will kneel humbly in front of a mirror, in order to dissolve completely into it. I will step into it—into a world where there are no words, no thoughts, no feelings, because there all parts are united once more in the indescribable Whole, triumphing over time and space, in the silence of All and Nothingness. There I will stand in the icy eternity of the gleaming eye.

And I am the eye!

When the constables of the magician come they will find nothing but a hollow shell, because I shall have freed myself from the world of words, over which Laurin reigns."

The End

14

AFTER THIS last entry in his journal Xaver Ykdrasil
Zangl stayed in his lodgings for almost another four weeks,
without the wide publicity, which the crime squad's searches
gained in the newspapers, leading to the police getting on to
his tracks. What went on inside him during these four weeks
we do not know, nor do we know what he did during that
time. Since neither neighbours nor local shopkeepers could
remember having seen him in the neighbourhood, we may
assume that he did not leave his lodgings again. According
to the statement made by his neighbour—the man Zangl
referred to when he said he had been in his apartment to
look for the judge's transmitter—it sometimes "got very
noisy" in Zangl's room, and presumably these noises were the
ones Zangl made when he smashed up his meagre furniture.
Because he must have gone berserk a few times, until he
became weaker and collapsed into the state of muzzy semi-
consciousness which he once described in his diary as paradise,
as "a corpse floating along twelve metres down" and then—
at the end—as a state of true individuality. It could not have
been possible to reach this condition without a lively revolt
of the natural life force against this violation, with which
this brilliant but disorientated mind sought to destroy itself.
One problem must have been hunger, as we can deduce from
the fact that Zangl tried to make a kind of porridge by
mixing paper, bits torn off the covers of books, and paint
scraped off the walls with water, and tried to swallow it,
until at the terminal phase, he was not even capable of this

crude but reasonable reaction and began to swallow his own excrement, when he was not using the handle of a spoon to smear it over the floor and the walls, and over himself as well, as neglected children sometimes do in their second year. No doubt this behaviour will have been commented on at length in the psychiatrist's report, so that I do not want to prolong the discussion here.

The general lack of interest evinced by the other occupants in the house as to what was going on behind Zangl's locked door is something of a riddle, because the inarticulate cries, the dull thudding noises and the fact that the lodger had not been seen for a long time, did not only suggest that he might need help, which the helpers might have found a nuisance and too much of a disruption of their everyday lives, but could have provoked protests about the noise, so that a local official could easily have been sent in to find out what was causing the noise behind the door.

Without knowing whether the commission is at all interested in this aspect of the case, I made some inquiries on the matter at the house, but all I got from the tenant living above Zangl was the following answer: "When the rumpus got goin' agin in the night," said the pensioner who lived up there, a track welder who used to be employed by the Viennese transport authority, "we used ter take a broom 'andle and thump on't floor. It warn't till they coom and took 'im orf in t'ambulance that I thought to mysel', 'appen somethin' warn't right. It 'ad bin all quiet like for two weeks afore that, and not a soul 'ad 'eard anythin' of 'im."

Several people in the house assured me that all they knew about Zangl's existence was the fact that there was no name plate on door number 17, although they knew a single, youngish man lived in there, who arrogantly refused to greet them. Unfortunately a lot of low types had moved in since the war, and it was better not to inquire into their private affairs. Like the case of old Mrs. Kwapil, who had died three years ago, the widow of a chief inspector in the press section of the police, so you see, it goes to show, a really posh lady who protested about the strong smell of potato stew which came from the new tenants in the neighbouring flat every day, whereupon someone unknown fed her dachshund Moffi on poisoned sausage and thus hastened the old lady's own passage to the grave with sorrow. Mrs. Kwapil's murderers had been of Hungarian origin, foreigners, like Zangl, who had also murdered, though not—thank God—in his own house.

I am only mentioning these details to the commission in order to make it clear to them that objective research into Zangl's social milieu, although revealing a large amount of information, does not make it possible to draw any useful conclusions other than the familiar one: that living in close physical contiguity alone does not effect the individual's integration into the social community, and that it is possible to die a more lonely death in a densely populated city area than anywhere else.

The fact that Zangl's death was only mental, and not physical, is due to purely material reasons which have absolutely nothing to do with any personal interest shown by any one human being to any other human being, and have nothing to do even with hostility or distrust, or any other negative motives. The fact was that Zangl, after paying the first month's rent when he moved in, had continued to owe further payments, so that the estate agent in the city which managed the house had instructed the manageress to deliver a written warning to the new tenant. This was the usual practice, the management informed me, since it had the advantage over postal delivery, in that the tenant who was behind with his rent would be afraid of getting into an argument with the manageress which might be overheard by the other tenants. In the face of this moral pressure most people chose to pay the deliverer of the warning on the spot. The addition of a warning in the prescribed postal fashion did shorten the legal interim required to get an eviction order, but Austrian laws regarding tenants' rights made trying to get an eviction order costly in terms of time and money, it was not easy to get a judgement and almost impossible to get it enforced. Hence the more humane way of direct human contact between the emissaries of the management and the tenant was preferable.

But in the case of Zangl this contact did not take place, since the manageress rang his bell several times to no avail, banged on the door and shouted and finally pushed the warning in a sealed envelope in the crack of the door just above the door handle, where it would be clearly visible to anyone returning home. The envelope stayed there for nearly a fortnight. Then the manageress reported that the warning could not be delivered by telephoning the estate agent, who decided that one should be sent by post. Only when it also proved impossible to deliver a registered or—to use the current jargon—"recorded delivery" letter and the manageress, in her monthly report to the estate agent, happened to mention in passing that it could not be assumed that the tenant had gone away, did the agent decide to have the door of the flat in the second courtyard, left staircase, third floor, door 17, opened by a reliable expert, namely, a locksmith from Area Five whom they usually employed for services of this kind. This decision was not taken lightly, as they anxiously assured me, but only after the manageress had been questioned for further details and it had been learned that a tenant who had met her on the stairs, which, she, the manageress, was just cleaning in punctual fulfilment of her duties, mentioned the fact that the tenant of number seventeen seemed to be just as much of a boozer and a rake as the rest of the mob that had moved in lately; when he was really drunk he sometimes made such a lot of noise that one might think he was smashing up his furniture, or worse.

The estate agent went to a lot of trouble to give me an

accurate picture of the state of affairs that had ultimately led to a decision to have the door opened. They obviously did not want me to conclude, from what they had told me, that the slightest shadow of blame could be attached to anyone, least of all the management and their employees. Because they did not know exactly the real aim and purpose of my investigation, because I had been able to avoid the confrontation of a direct question, thanks to my decisive manner. Although, in so far as I understand the instructions of the committee, I am not expected to produce material, as a result of my researches, which would justify taking action in the legal sense against either management or tenants, so that I could easily have explained this, I was convinced that it would help to make my report more complete if I let the people argue away. And one could only expect them to be anxious to talk if they remained in the dark about the goal of my inquiry and if their admittedly underlying but nevertheless bad consciences made them try to meet any conceivable reproaches in advance. No doubt it was also their bad consciences that stopped them from asking me for my credentials. For the time being I myself did not understand the origin of this useful bad conscience, but since I became aware of it, to my astonishment, within the first five minutes of my visit to the estate agent, I made cautious use of it. I phrased my quesions with just the right amount of mild sharpness, which did not let them feel a concealed indictment, but simply made the person questioned feel the need to squash any dawning suspicion in good time, which would precede an indictment, before it could crystallise to a seed of suspicion. If my manner had been just a little more sharp, I would have provoked just the opposite reaction, namely, self-defence in the form of aggression against myself, perhaps in the form of a question, who I really was and what gave me the right to put questions, answering which involved an unreasonable demand on the estate agent's valuable time.

But as it was, after a brief glance at my visiting card which gave my profession as "Investigator", I was asked to take a seat in an armchair, I was given a small cup of Turkish coffee, for which I thanked them politely, as I did for their kindness in offering to co-operate, I was shown the contract for Zangl's lease, which revealed—as was pointed out to me—amongst other things, that the tenant had paid no more than a moderate and customary amount of key-money, it's moderate size being all the more defensible in that the accommodation in question had had the door-jamb and window frames painted only ten years ago, and the water heater above the sink had also been repaired; in short, everything was done to set my mind at rest, and at the same time to strengthen their own conviction that they had nothing, absolutely nothing to reproach themselves with where Zangl was concerned, that in fact, they had behaved in a thoroughly decent manner and had fulfilled all moral and legal obligations.

When I left I reiterated my thanks and assured them that I had found everything most reassuring. They thanked me very warmly and invited me to make use of their services at any time.

After my visit to the estate agent I wondered for a long time about the reason for the underlying bad conscience I had detected. I found an explanation which I do not want to withhold from the commission, even if I do run the risk of leaving the firm ground of reality and giving the impression of an uncritical speculator. The danger of laying myself open to the accusation of groundless speculation was one I started to run the moment I began to describe my visit to the estate agent in such detail, without leaving out any subjective evaluation of the behaviour of the person I was talking to. But how could I otherwise have described my visit in a mean-ingful and convincing way, if not through my subjective appraisal?

A so-called objective description would have revealed nothing more than the fact that Zangl, shortly before his physical death, was found by one of the locksmiths employed by the management, because the management wanted to make use of their contractual right to inspect the dwelling of a tenant who was in arrears, in order to find out how they could get their money and avoid further losses.

But this information is not sufficient for us if we want to penetrate the deeper background of the Zangl case—to find an answer, at this point in my report, as to how it was possible for Zangl to waste away for almost four weeks in total isolation, although he raved and screamed and smashed his furniture, without these powerful acoustic signals drawing any rescuers. If one wants to obtain an answer to this question, which is closely connected to the question of Zangl's relationship with his environment, I must be permitted to leave the ground of superficial reality and adopt subjective evaluations in the topics we are now considering. My subjective evaluation might well, after all, be elevated to the rank of objective and tangible reality, if the gentlemen at the estate agents's office could undergo a psychiatric examination to establish whether they really did have an underlying bad conscience in connection with the case of Zangl, or whether they were always in the habit of giving detailed answers at any time to anyone who put questions to them, so that their friendly manner towards me was only the overflowing, unselfish helpfulness which they showed to everyone, a willingness to be helpful which made them fulfill any request, whether there was any profit to be had from it or not. So the analysis I made intuitively would have to be repeated by psychiatric means, which the commission are hardly able to do. Why should the estate agents allow themselves to be examined by a psychiatrist? They would indignantly reject any such demand, not only because it would represent a probably unpleasant interference in the legally protected sphere of their private lives, but also and above all because they would undoubtedly feel themselves unjustly attacked, namely, accused of some sort of guilty involvement in the case of the mentally deranged murderer, Xaver Ykdrasil Zangl.

Should the commission be drawn to certain conclusions by my report, and then compress these conclusions into the suggestion that certain inferences could be drawn, affecting our laws or administration, perhaps in the area of social hygiene, or at least give cause for sociological research, my supposition, based on subjective intuition, that the building manager had shown a latent tendency to a bad conscience from the start, would enter the world of incontrovertible realities. This would even be the case if my report was taken as no more than an attempt to contribute to the striving of science to discover the basic laws and method of human knowledge: namely, the process whereby my perception projects thought structures on to the surrounding world and then recognises the surrounding world with the help of this projection, so that in the last analysis there is no such thing as objective and probable reality, so that all the things we know are equally true and false, according to whether we are prepared to recognise the underlying thought structures or not. This way of looking at things does unfortunately mean the painful rejection of the assumption we so dearly love to make, namely, the existence of a recognisable absolute. On the other hand we gain the moral freedom to project new thought structures into our world—thought structures that might have the advantage of our being able to create a more harmonious world picture than the one left to us by our fathers.

I ask the commission's forgiveness for this digression into the realms of philosophy and hurry to return to the object of my labours, but not without expressing the request that, in considering the case of Zangl as a result of my report, the philosophical speculation contained in my digression should be adopted as a working hypothesis, at least in passing, since it happens to be the thought structure that I have projected on to the reality of the Zangl case, on this chaos of murder and reason.

What conclusion can we draw, therefore, from the fact that the housing management betrayed a bad conscience in connection with this case?

As I have already said, this bad conscience is not really present at all as yet, but impels the manager's being as a latent tendency in his subconscious. It is an undefined bad conscience, which could manifest itself here one minute, there the next, perhaps in the feeling, that the legality of having the apartment opened might be doubtful, or at least, even if justified in itself, could be doubtful, given dubious side-factors.

The person who opened the door, for example, could represent such a dubious side-factor, which was why they hurriedly emphasised his proven reliability. Or the date when the door was opened could be open to criticism, for example, it could have been done too late, or, on the other hand, prematurely. The possibility of justified criticism was also sensed by the managers on everything to do with the manageress of the house: on the one hand the fact that she gossiped on the stairs, on the other hand her negligence in reporting to the agent, when she was not gossipy enough; the fact that in one of the houses managed by this management, a human drama of such magnitude could take place unnoticed, right under the nose of the person in charge; furthermore, the fact that one of the tenants considered him a boozer and a rake, when it was more a question of mental illness, and the fact that boozers and rakes should be tolerated at all in a house that they managed. The lease that they had contracted with Zangl also occasioned unease: perhaps it was legally correct, but possibly open to criticism in connection with the key-money Zangl had paid, a fact that did perhaps disclose a wicked swindle, or, under closer examination, might

have revealed obvious and illegal manipulation on the part
of the manager, perhaps an offence against the law on rent-
ing, or the taking of bribes, not booked so as to avoid taxa-
tion, which had flowed directly into the manager's pocket
in an illegal fashion.

In short, contact with Zangl, which in the first instance
was nothing more than one of many everyday occurrences
in connection with his work, as far as the housing manager
was concerned, revealed itself afterwards as a relationship
full to the brim with possibilities, as yet abstract, for becoming guilty. No, not for becoming guilty, but for having
become guilty afterwards. Surely there is an alarming simi-
larity between the manager's situation when I visited him
and the situation, which Zangl himself described, of the child
under the motionless gaze of a merciless and silent law court?

For the moment the role of the court of law was being
played for the manager by myself, as the investigator, but it
is a role that the producer can swap about as he pleases,
tomorrow it can be played by a member of the commission,
the day after tomorrow by a tax inspector or a relative of
Zangl's appearing with the complaint that some valuable
belonging to the occupant had disappeared when the flat was
opened.

The role, as I have said, can be played by different people,
but the medium through which this role made its prominent
appearance in the manager's life—this medium has an obvious
identity: it is the person of Zangl, through the change that
came over his role as far as the manager was concerned,
namely, the role of anonymous tenant to begin with, but
then it suddenly switched to the role of the strange, the out-
of-the-ordinary, the unforeseen, everything out of the normal
run of things, murder and madness, which, for the manager,
as for the rest of the city, represents evil, in fact satisfies the
need for evil. For the manager, Zangl did not only play the
role of a management problem, which only concerned him

personally, which could be solved by sending, first a warning, then a locksmith, but also the role of evil, which permitted one to point a finger at the player, so that one apparently localised the evil, looked at it squarely, so as to reassure oneself that it was outside oneself and therefore not within one. And this creates a connection between me and the manager, so that on the one hand I remind the manager of the evil inside himself, while he tries to nullify what he might regard as the growing danger of my role with an assurance about our fellowship, a fellowship which springs from the fact that Zangl is the rejected evil one, whilst we two are members of the protective society of good people. The cup of coffee and his helpfulness in giving information is the form his oath of allegiance takes, and he uses it to try and avert the danger I represent.

The manager's involvement with Zangl goes deeper, because as the figure representing evil, purely and simply, Zangl does not only liberate the manager from the pressure of evil, he is also, in spite of superficial and gladly accepted differences, basically related to him—a relationship which leads to the responsibility of one for the other. Zangl had carried out his part of this responsibility by allowing a terrible guilt to be projected on to him—but the manager? What had he done for Zangl? This question, honoured members of the commission, is the key to the whole riddle as to why the estate agents were so friendly and co-operative.

15

IF THE COMMISSION have followed me patiently up till now, they will understand why I spent so much time describing and commenting on my visit to the estate agent, when I am sure some members of the commission would have liked more "reality", for example, an account of the result of my researches with regard to Xaver Ykdrasil's mother and his former wife. I did in fact manage to trace the latter, and the thorough interview I had with her revealed a certain amount of further material, which also provides information about the sort of person Zangl's mother was and the picture that this courageous woman had of her son shortly before her death. I even saw Zangl's own son, apparently a very healthy boy physically, of pre-school age. But I consider it superfluous to include this material in my report, damaging in fact, since it would need further comments before it could be made comprehensible to the commission. I would request the commission not to regard this assertion as any attempt on my part to browbeat the commission, I make it in the same spirit as I also allowed myself to mention my visit to the estate agent.

My report already holds such a lot of unprepared material, I have already given so many bare facts that the addition of more such unanalysed material would only cloud our vision again, when I have just hoped to clarify it with my description of the state of affairs in the estate agent's office. That I have chosen to improve our vision by analytical comments on a situation which I know a lot about as one of the participants, should not be ascribed to a vain desire on my part to push myself into the foreground, but as an indication of particular care, since this care was necessary to be able to draw the convincing conclusion which I personally did draw from my investigation of the Zangl case. The conclusion is, that relationships between human beings depend on the usefulness of these relationships to the people involved—not just the superficial, material usefulness, but a usefulness related to the area of subconscious emotions, resulting from the fact that one person plays a role for another and becomes the bearer of a projection. The relationship of Zangl to Dr. Kralicek and to his two victims depends on projection; but it would be a mistake to assume that the projection was entirely on Zangl's side, and that he dictated the roles to these people.

Since they were also prepared to form some sort of connection with Zangl, I am sure that they also threw their psychic image on to him and used him as a projective surface. What projective possibilities Dr. Kralicek sensed in this patient can only be vaguely guessed at, since we lack any information on the doctor's psychic structure, but I would like to repeat the hint I gave earlier, that Kralicek had an aggressive impulse towards neurotically disturbed patients as a result of a feeling of envy; that, in addition, Zangl was an object of attraction to the doctor for reasons of professional pride, since he could try himself out as a specialist on him, without having to become aware of it.

The professional ethics of the doctor anchored in his everyday consciousness, would never have allowed him to continue his contact with Zangl if he had clearly recognised that, by the form that his contacts took, he was far overstepping the limits of his professional capacity. But Zangl's unusual personal situation allowed Kralicek to satisfy his forbidden longing to extend his professional field of action and to convince himself at the same time that he was just doing a patient a kindness in an unselfish way. In actual fact Kralicek may suffer from a deeply suppressed inferiority complex, which drives him constantly to seek reassurance about himself in his dealings with the outside world.

Unfortunately we know absolutely nothing about the psychic structure of the one in green, but Zangl may—like every other customer—have played the role of the humiliator and besmircher for her, since many prostitutes come to their profession because of psychological masochism, which is satisfied by the notion that they are the outcasts of society. On this point I refer the reader to the entry in Zangl's diary on the subject of the Japanese sect. If the one in green saw the humiliator and besmircher in Zangl, from whom she wanted to get pleasurable confirmation of the feeling of being rejected, then she had come to the wrong address as far as Zangl was concerned, because he was looking for contact with what was generally considered low in her, and came begging at her feet instead of using her contemptuously, like any passer-by, and then leaving her. In Zangl's minutely described account of this encounter we learned how both partners fought bitterly to make the other play the role intended for him, or her. Finally the one in green left Zangl resignedly, to look for a customer who would not question her role, whilst Zangl's subconscious refused to abandon the established contact without making some use of it and hastily discovered another role for the one in green, namely, the personification of evil, by the destruction of which he could free himself from the tormenting impulse of having to want anything to do with her.

The fact that Zangl often had several roles ready for the people within his sphere and hastily changed his projections on to people is only, in my opinion, because, owing to his isolation, he had too little human material at his disposal, on to which he could throw his projections.

We have learned from Zangl's sensitive description of his

feelings that he was always filled with pleasurable emotion, the feeling that he was really alive, really existed, when he had succeeded in a projection long denied him: after his first contact with the doctor, after the murder of the one in green, on his way to the judge and even more so after he had killed him—each time he feels free, elated, creative, quite at home in this world. And now let us extend the argument beyond Zangl's immediate circle to the estate agent: what emotion did the manager show, when I indicated to him, in the course of my conversation with him, that nobody was quarrelling with the projections he desired, that everyone would play their roles just as he had arranged? He was elated, jovial, genial and ready to be helpful. Having carefully brought my argument to this point I do not wish to maintain that absolutely every relationship, whether it is the relationship between a married couple or one between parents and children, the relationship between a superior manager and a concierge or that between doctor and patient, even the anonymous relationships within a city community and a state, is based on a projection of roles, which has its imperative in dormant structures deep inside human beings.

The individuality of each person, in this closely knit web of abstract emotional and behavioural patterns which is usually referred to as the social reality of any one society, is defined by the superimposition of many roles. So the individual personality could be compared to a knot in a fishing net —any attempt to cut it out of the net and isolate it as a concept of knot results in it vanishing altogether.

And it was this that Xaver Ykdrasil Zangl experienced for himself: he isolated himself more and more from the social web, in order to be able to question everything that appeared to stand in the way of discovering what he assumed to be his own individuality; but all he achieved this way was the total loss of his individuality. Today he is vegetating in the closed ward of a state mental hospital, abandoned—in a way that his consciousness can no longer control—to the drives of his vegetative nervous system, in the dark and icy loneliness in which we would all live if we did not make a world of men from the chaos of reality by projecting the structures dormant inside us.

Where can we ascribe blame, in this tragedy of Xaver Ykdrasil Zangl? We can only inquire after the causes which led to alterations in the web of structures round about Zangl and in Zangl himself, admittedly without any hope of a satisfactory answer. Because the mysterious dark side that forced Zangl into isolation and which manifested itself both in a Faustian thirst for knowledge and in a low search for obscenity, will remain intangible to us so long as we do not know the psychic patterns of the social landscape which was once Zangl's home and which is still our home.

Now that I have finished the work of investigation into the Zangl case, I realise that the only meaningful question in the whole case, namely the question about the nature and cause of the dark side in Zangl's life, could only have been solved if I could have conducted the investigation, not from the person of Zangl himself, and then moving outward in ever wider circles, but had started from the whole of our contemporary reality and moved in ever narrower circles towards Zangl.

Since, in asking me to undertake this work, the commission did not tell me exactly what answer they wished to hear, I can only close the report with the assertion, that I am unable to give any answer.